Evan

was young, almost pitifully young, to have seen and done so much, and to have been running so long. Now he had his airplane ticket in his pocket. Now he was going home to a country he had fled, and to a fate he could no longer avoid.

Dierdre

was used to the eyes of every man and woman following her as she entered a room. Her face and figure were famous, her clothes fabulous, her life-style free as the wind. What no one could see was the emptiness within her, filled only with the pain of the past and dread of the future.

They both knew love was not for them. They both knew they were wrong for each other. Then they found out how little they really knew....

A ROBERT WISE PRODUCTION

"TWO PEOPLE"

starring

Peter Fonda
Lindsay Wagner
Estelle Parsons

Written by
RICHARD DEROY

Produced and Directed by
ROBERT WISE

From The FILMAKERS GROUP
A UNIVERSAL PICTURE

TECHNICOLOR®

Two People

ALICE BOYD

based on the screenplay by Richard DeRoy

A DELL BOOK

Published by
Dell Publishing Co., Inc.
1 Dag Hammarskjold Plaza
New York, New York 10017

Printed in the United States of America
First printing—March 1973
Second printing—June 1973

1

IT WOULD EITHER be a letter—official, heavily embossed, and sealed—or a person: a man, also heavy and official, who would knock on his door, or call pompously from below: "Evan Bonner!"

More likely a letter.

Evan shifted about on his bed, the bed that was harder and narrower than an army cot and which at the moment was covered with letters, none of them official or very new.

Blond and blue-eyed, he was the type of youth that appears on the slopes at Aspen or Stowe or in the surf at La Jolla or Waikiki far more often than in seedy rooms in North Africa. And although his face showed considerable tension and strain and some hurt, it was still an open face with an honest American capacity for happiness and amusement. A look that once was called "clean-cut." There was also a certain strength in his face, a strength beyond simple physical well-being: the strength of a man, however young, who knew his own mind, who had found his center of gravity.

The room in which Evan waited, and thought,

was small, with one high window and a narrow, low-beamed door. At one time that space might have been a cube; now the worn floor boards had sunk lopsidedly, and the ceiling had sagged in another direction. At first Evan, who was in many ways a nice American boy, well brought-up, had scrubbed the plaster walls, but some darkness had seeped back onto them so that now his efforts had the shape of continents, with unknown areas in shade. Through the window sometimes came the throbbing, frantic sounds of the outside city that was Marrakesh—sounds and a city that were no longer exotic or even interesting to Evan. It was a city that had come to seem the end of the world to him, as his room seemed an ultimate—or perhaps penultimate—prison.

He shifted again, leaning up on an elbow, and chose a letter: blue, in his mother's tidy, rounded hand. He read: "I can't remember when spring has been as late as it is this year. The ground stays hard from the frost. The trees look black and I keep waiting for leaves and some green to show. We have Garden Club meetings but they seem sort of silly, with no flowers in sight. I still hope that you can come home soon."

Evan smiled a little sadly at his mother's affection and at her transparentness, and he thought: Mother, even if I could come home I might not bring spring weather.

The second letter, from the oldest of his three sisters said: "I might as well tell you what I think." As though she had never before told a

6

thought. "I think you just aren't thinking clearly. Just because rebellion is very *in* this year. I suppose you've got a beard and all the rest of the trappings. I remember in high school you looked so clean even when you'd just come in from a game."

He put that one down quickly and took up another. His friend Gordon in Canada. "It's really kind of neat here, but not in all ways, you know? I mean, I really like the country, *really*, but sometimes when Cat's asleep I wonder about ten years from now, what will we be doing then? I can't get work, and how long can we live on her waitress job? Well, I guess I could wonder anywhere. But man, I still wish you'd come with us."

Evan sighed and took up the last: a tiny, faintly flowered note from lovely blonde Nora in Stockholm. "I decided that you were right. It was never love with us, just sympathy. Now that I have met Max I see the difference."

Evan gave a wry smile to that one and thought: Good luck to you, Nora, with Max and then with whomever else comes along and teaches you about true love.

Then, to shake off the effect of his letters, he stood up and looked at his watch. He could, if he wanted to, go out for his mail. Or he could go tomorrow or the day after tomorrow. In any case, his was a full-time wait—for unwelcome letters, for unknown visitors. Months ago—he had almost lost track of how many—he had imagined the letter that would come: its thunderous conclusive sentences. Or the man: the heavy stalwart neck that supported an upright head, a small emblem in the blue serge buttonhole. But by now his curiosity had almost disappeared; he had nearly stopped thinking about either the message or the man.

Standing in the middle of the room—he could have touched any wall or reached the ceiling—Evan made a gesture that had become so automatic he no longer knew when he performed it: he lifted his chin and stretched his neck around, first to one side and then another, at the same time extending his arms, clenching and unclenching his fists.

By the time that was over he had decided to stay where he was. He lay back on his bed, having had a sudden and insistent premonition that today would be the day when something happened.

2

ON NO STREET in the United States would Fitzgerald have appeared remarkable; he had, in fact, a quality of merging into landscapes, or rather into cityscapes—a quality of anonymity. He was vaguely handsome in an average, not-striking way. About thirty, he was sad-eyed, firm of mouth. His clothes were good but a little shabby: pockets of the tweed coat stretched and sagging, shoes run down at the heels. Impossible to guess his occupation, marital status, or anything else about him.

But in the Jamaa El-Fina, a gigantic open square in the heart of Marrakesh, just outside the walls of the native quarter, Fitzgerald's very colorlessness made him remarkable. Not that anyone noticed: there was too much else to see. In fact a busload of tourists, who had just arrived, gazed about in a sort of stupor: so much to photograph —how not to waste a shot?

The Jamaa is many things: a depot for caravans from the Sahara; an outsized market, a social center for the poor of Marrakesh—the loafers, the laborers, the children, the endless variety of passive onlookers who take their places in the sun there every afternoon. It is a circus with more than a hundred rings.

On the afternoon that Fitzgerald began his necessarily slow walk across the square, there was the usual surging throng. Moroccans, Tunisians, black Africans. Nomad tribesmen in their dusty, ancient robes; farmers; city men in djellabas or dark serge "western" suits. And among the thousands of Africans there was perhaps a handful of American tourists, in twos and threes, guided through the throng by darting native urchins.

Fitzgerald was clearly not a tourist. He had the unobservant stare of a man in very familiar surroundings and the steady pace of a man with a mission.

A circle of watchers was mesmerized as a fire-eater swallowed flames, his head held back, mouth lifted to receive the fire. Three Senegalese princesses, black Amazons swathed in orange, paused to watch two performing wrestlers. There were rebad vendors and water sellers, snake charmers, and above them all the remote figure of a Berber tribesman, borne aloft on a camel. A scribe sat cross-legged on the ground in front of his ancient typewriter, while a veiled Arab woman, seated beside him, dictated a letter. A troup of fierce white-robed male dancers pranced by. Then a pack of garrulous black businessmen, up from the Cameroons, suited and fezzed for a local convention perhaps or a celebration.

Eschewing caution, the bedazzled Germans

clicked their expensive cameras at everything—
even, by mistake, at Fitzgerald. Later they would
turn the pages of their tidy albums and wonder
who that American was: a commercial traveler? a
minor diplomat? a spy?

The noise was thunderous: the din of a thousand voices shouting in a hundred dialects, shrill
percussions of roaming musicians, the ritual spiels
of the vendors, the preachers, the storytellers.
Superimposed on all this was the inevitable wail
of transistor radios, elaborating on the din with
staccato Arab newscasts or the music of exotic
reeds. Or American rock.

And the smells: dust and flowers, incense and
camel dung, human excrement and sweat. The
smells of excitement and of poverty.

Fitzgerald threaded his way through the packed
square, passing a group that surrounded a story-
teller, skirting the crowd around a troupe of acro-
bats. He continued through the thick of that tumult until he reached the edge of the square.
Then, passing the artisans and their stalls and a
camel caravan that had come to rest, he continued
on, away from the Jamaa, into the street that led
into the native quarter—the Medina.

On that street heavy traffic, both pedestrian and
vehicular, moved swiftly in and out of the Medina.
Fitzgerald stepped back to avoid being hit by a
speeding mini-cab. A moment later, a caleche bore
down on him from the opposite direction, its lone
passenger a veiled Arab woman. As it passed, all
but grazing his shoulder, Fitzgerald did not even

look up. He walked on past grocers' shops, notions stores, butchers' and produce stalls, past a dentist's shop—announced by a dirty display of dentures in an outside case—from which there issued a moan of pain. Fitzgerald grinned slightly and continued on.

Along the sides of the street were dozens of shops displaying the same assortment of brass and silvery trays, tea services, vases. The air was punctuated with sounds of hammers on metal. From time to time artisans appeared in the stalls, to stamp out a pattern on a piece. Sometimes a brass merchant would try, generally without success, to lure a tourist into his shop. Fitzgerald passed on, ignored by the merchants; instinctively they knew a local.

He walked beneath a canopy of drying yarns, giant skeins of yellows and reds that transformed the squalid street into a panoply of brilliant color. Then he turned into an alley, pressing himself to the wall to allow a donkey cart to pass, its platform piled with raw wool for the dyers. Once the cart was past, Fitzgerald moved along into the alley.

He came out then into a residential street, narrow, shadowed, walled by high houses. In that street children played; groups of schoolgirls in European dress. Marrakesh housewives, prosaic despite their veils, clacked their high heels on the stones beneath their dull gray caftans, bringing home their marketing: native breads side by side with American boxed detergents in string shopping bags.

Reaching another alley, Fitzgerald stopped to read a marker on the wall, then turned into the alley. This alley was a tortuous crevice between more houses. It was deathly silent except for the distant sounds from the Medina—as if Fitzgerald had stepped literally into another world. He walked on into the silence; occasionally he passed a solitary Arab, hunching along with a cane, or a sad thin stray cat. Finally he stopped at a house and took a slip of paper from his pocket. He checked the house number and tried the door. Finding it open, he went through a low-ceilinged passage that brought him into a shabby courtyard. He stopped and looked up, studying the fringed and rusted balconies.

Then suddenly, as though she had materialized from the shadows in the corners of the courtyard, a young Arab girl appeared at his side—filthy, but somewhat prettier than she was dirty.

Speaking perfect Arabic—languages were among his disguises—Fitzgerald told her that he was looking for Mr. Bonner.

But the girl shook her head. He might have been speaking Chinese.

"Mr. Evan Bonner," Fitzgerald said.

And now the girl answered in Arabic. "There is no Mr. Bonner here."

"Tell him that Mr. Fitzgerald is here."

"I don't know Mr. Bonner." The girl stared at

him incuriously—very much the same stare he might have given her, had they passed in the Jamaa.

"This is very stupid," Fitzgerald said.

The girl answered with a bland silence.

Then, from an obscure upper balcony came a very American voice. "Fitzgerald?"

"Bonner?"

The disembodied voice continued from the shadowed balcony. "I figured you'd write me a letter."

Fitzgerald stood impassively in the square, in full view, speaking into the shadows. "I'm here in Marrakesh for the day. On something else."

The voice now came from a somewhat lower level, a very American and very young voice, but one not lacking in authority. "What did you say?"

Speaking loudly to emphasize the point Fitzgerald said, "I had to come anyway."

The voice of Evan Bonner became tentative as he asked, "Are you alone?"

"Yes." And then, "There's no reason for me not to be, you know."

A moment's hesitation. "Sure."

After that came a long silence, broken only by the sound of Evan's hesitant footsteps descending the stairs, echoing across the courtyard.

The Arab girl had retreated to a distance some yards from Fitzgerald, but she continued to stand there, facing the direction that he faced, as though she were waiting with him. A tiny child, barely walking and even dirtier than she was, came out from the corner shadows and stood beside her. She took his hand protectively; he could have been her brother, or her son.

For a moment longer Fitzgerald stood listening to the footsteps. Then, as he saw Evan emerge from the stairwell into the courtyard, Fitzgerald for the first time that day reacted visibly: he had obviously expected another sort of boy.

The two men looked at each other with a curiosity that was not unfriendly. Evan spoke first, with a small grin. "I expected someone older," he said.

Fitzgerald smiled. "Fat neck? Rotary button?"

"Something like that."

"Sorry." He hesitated. "You're not exactly what I had in mind either."

Evan's grin increased. "No beard?"

Fitzgerald admitted, "Among other things."

At that moment the baby freed himself from the girl and ran unsteadily over to the wall to urinate.

The girl screamed at him in Arabic. "Shame on you. You disgrace the house with your filth!"

The two men exchanged faint smiles, as though this performance had been for their benefit—as perhaps it was.

Looking around the square and then at Evan, Fitzgerald asked if there was somewhere they could talk. "How about your room?"

"My room's pretty crummy."

"Well then—back to the Jamaa?"

"Okay with me."

From the roof garden of the CTM Hotel, high above the Jamaa, one can see the square ramparts of Marrakesh and the distant slopes of the Atlas mountains. As though he had not seen them before, Evan stared out to the range, from his table by the balustrade.

At the next table a flank of the inevitable German tourists, their light meters bouncing against their chests, leaned out precariously to focus their cameras on the market below. The Germans mopped their brows; they swilled their beer as they recorded the exotic scene for future evenings in Dusseldorf.

Carrying two large cokes, Fitzgerald made his way, between the Germans and the crowds of black businessmen that thronged the roof, toward the table.

"Here." Placing the drinks he sat down.

"Thanks." Then, with blue-eyed directness, Evan asked, "When can I leave?"

Fitzgerald had been expecting the question, and his voice became dry and informative. "There are nonstops from Casablanca to New York. But the next one isn't till Monday."

Evan spoke quickly and firmly. "I don't want to wait."

Fitzgerald softened. "Then go by way of Paris," he said. "Any day. We pay the fare."

"Can you get me a ticket for tomorrow?" Still with the directness that many people found quite unnerving.

But Fitzgerald spoke lightly. "If you like. The train for Casablanca leaves around seven-thirty in the morning. Ungodly hour."

Looking for a moment back to the mountains, Evan said, "It doesn't matter. Actually I haven't been sleeping too well." A quick smile erased any possible self-pity from the statement.

Just then a noisy altercation began at the adjacent table. Two large red-faced men, one in lederhosen, the other in heavy twill, began to shout across the table at each other. Standing up, they flourished indistinguishable banknotes at one another in an argument over who was to pay the check—or rather, who was to have the privilege of playing host. Somehow, it was finally settled, and their strident voices faded into the general cafe din once again.

When Fitzgerald spoke it was obvious that he had been considering his thought. He was, in fact, a man who considered most thoughts before giving voice to them. "Look," he said, "why don't you have dinner with me tonight?" And then, quickly, "Or is there someone you—someone you want to be with?"

"No. There isn't." Evan's reply was unambiguous but faintly sad.

Fitzgerald asked, "How long have you been here?"

"Quite a while." And then the grin that was almost but not quite "wholesome," appeared as Evan said, "Thanks, I could use a good meal."

3

THE GHARNATTA RESTAURANT, once the reception room of a palace, could only be described as magnificent. Tiled, with vaulted alcoves that surround a brilliant mosaic floor. Sophisticated crystal light fixtures, and arabesque-patterned stucco with cedar beams. The room could hardly be more appealing to a westerner's sense of the exotic, the marvelous.

An unromatic combination in that most romantic place, Fitzgerald and Evan sat at a low table, eating couscous from ornate brass serving dishes. The other diners, a noisy French group and a few very sedate African couples, seemed far more conscious of their surroundings. The others looked around and exclaimed; Evan and Fitzgerald had an air of keeping to business.

Pushing back a little from the table, Evan asked, "Will someone be waiting for me in New York?"

"I don't think so, but I'm not sure. I'll give you an address."

Waitresses in brilliant harem garb, with golden

ankle bracelets gleaming, brought yet another course to the hungry French. More steaming plates, more wine.

Fitzgerald studied Evan a moment and then said, "Bonner, can I ask you something?" The question came out with some intensity.

Evan looked up, waiting.

"Why did you do it?"

Evan thought for a moment, but he answered simply, "I didn't like the alternatives."

Fitzgerald nodded, understanding. "I can't say that I blame you. But how do you feel now?"

"About what's coming?"

Fitzgerald nodded again. "Yes."

Evan had begun to sound tired. "I wrote to you, didn't I?"

For a moment they ate in silence, then Evan asked, "You like what you do?"

"I like the places. Moving around." This was said quite directly, without forethought.

"Where have you been?"

"Geneva for three years . . . Buenos Aires . . . Moscow." Then he interrupted himself, as though from a reverie, and said abruptly, "I have your tickets."

He took an envelope from inside his jacket and handed it to Evan.

In the dim candlelight Evan glanced at the airline ticket. "First class?"

Fitzgerald shrugged. "I thought you might as well be comfortable."

"How did you write this one off?" Evan teased.

By way of an answer, Fitzgerald asked, "Do you need any money?"

"No, that's okay."

Diffidently Fitzgerald added, "I can always arrange it."

Evan laughed, he knew better. "From your own pocket?"

"Does it matter?"

They regarded each other for a moment, both curious and, on the whole, kindly disposed toward one another.

Wryly Evan broke the silence. "You're a good man, Fitzgerald."

The answer was as wry. "Just don't tell my employers."

Down below, in a narrow alley in the Medina, which was silent except for the wail of a radio, an urchin led three Americans toward the Gharnatta Restaurant. A man and two women. Groping through the dark, their progress was so slow that the urchin had to pace himself: he moved ahead a few steps, stopped to wait for them, moved ahead, stopped, and hoped that his tip would make it all worthwhile.

The man, whose languid stroll was delaying both the urchin and the two women who followed, was Ron Kesselman, thirtyish, sandy-haired, very handsome. Deirdre McCluskey, a tall and beautiful young woman, a dark blonde with dark blue eyes, came next, taking great care not to brush against or in any way touch Ron. Bringing up the rear was Barbara Newman. Barbara, a few years ago, had been a softly pretty woman, but now she had the harassed, intelligent look that befitted a busy fashion editor.

Barbara stumbled against Deirdre. She muttered a quick apology as she looked around Deirdre to ask, "Ron, couldn't we walk a little faster?"

"He never hurries," Deirdre said. "You lose grace if you hurry." A well-known model, even her voice had an attractive surface.

Ron smiled, but he smiled as though the joke were on someone else. Barbara frowned uncomfortably.

The sumptuous illuminated entrance of the Gharnatta appeared ahead and the urchin pointed and gestured, urging them toward it. He opened the door for them, making a small bow to each.

"I will wait for you," he announced in his somewhat rough street French.

"Will you eat?" Barbara's French was collegiate —Hunter College, 1953—but well intended.

The boy nodded, and Barbara restrained an impulse to pat his shoulder as the three of them entered the restaurant.

An imposing trio: Deirdre magnificent in orange, a long orange chenille coat that covered her orange silk dress, and orange-dyed ostrich feathers that framed her face. Barbara striking in her full-length black, with a gaudy scarf. Ron in expensive imitation-safari clothes.

Their host rushed over to greet them, his

French more fluent that either the urchin's or Barbara's. "Good evening—good evening! And welcome to Gharnatta!"

Ron and Deirdre smiled gracefully, as Barbara said that it was lovely, they were enchanted.

"Thank you—if you'll come this way?"

And he led them proudly across the room toward an alcove.

Everyone stared as they crossed the floor, and one person recognized them. "Hello there," said Fitzgerald.

"Why hello!" Barbara started toward his table, whispering to Deirdre, "It's that nice Mr. Fitzgerald from Rabat."

Fitzgerald got up, and said hello again.

Deirdre smiled at him; a good smile, not one of her professional "Specials." "I like your country," she said. "You want to trade?"

Out of shyness, and some other reluctance that he did not understand, Evan had remained seated. He was staring at Deirdre. Sure that he had never seen her before, still Evan *recognized* this girl; he felt her presence, he sensed her being with a force that was almost painful. At that moment she turned to him, having clearly felt his stare, and they exchanged a look that was long and serious.

"Stay a while," Fitzgerald said to Deirdre.

She tore her gaze from Evan. "Ron's finished shooting. We're leaving tomorrow," she told Fitzgerald.

Fitzgerald muttered a regretful, "What a pity."

Abruptly, as though she had seen something

that was in some way unwelcome, Deirdre turned and started toward their table. She was followed by Ron.

"We'd love to stay," said Barbara. "Really we would."

And after a further exchange of smiles, she followed Deirdre and Ron to their alcove.

Not quite casually, Evan asked Fitzgerald, "Who's that girl?"

"You don't recognize her?"

"No. Not really. I should?"

"She's a fashion model. I thought you'd know her face. But of course it's of pretty recent fame."

Evan looked over toward the trio in their alcove. "Good-looking girl."

Fitzgerald followed his glance. "I have a hunch that she's also nice," he said. And then, as though he had gone too far, he added dryly, "They've been shooting all over Morocco. This country's being photographed to death."

A few moments later, from his own thoughts, Evan said, "She looks haunted. Or maybe just hurt."

Gently Fitzgerald commented, "You *are* a romantic."

"I guess."

Across the room a waiter, costumed in scarlet turban, scarlet tunic over tights, began to set places for the other Americans.

With exaggerated nonchalance, Ron announced, "I've decided what I'm going to do tomorrow, you know? I'm going to go to the Sahara."

Deirdre's look was one of controlled dislike. "Don't you think you should get back to New York?"

He looked around the room silently before answering; once, long ago, he had been told that silence is sexy. Then, slowly and more than a little provocatively, he said, "I think I should go to the Sahara. Why don't you come with me?"

Softly, wearily, Deirdre said, "I don't want to."

"You can fly to New York on Monday."

"I don't want to wait."

As happens with people who have quarreled often, they both sounded a little bored, but they were unable to stop.

"Why not?" Ron asked.

She lashed out. "You know perfectly well why not!" The surface of her voice had broken, giving her reply a harsh low tone. The French people stared.

Pleased, Ron looked at her for a moment. Then he turned to Barbara. "Why don't you come, Barbara. The desert? The stars? We can ravish each other." The passive drawl was subtly insulting, but Ron's half-conscious theory was that passivity rendered him guiltless.

Barbara responded by smiling uncomfortably and watching the waiter, but it was all too familiar to Deirdre, who burst out sharply, "Is she supposed to think that's funny? *Or* endearing?"

Barbara looked nervously from one to the

other. "Now if you two are going to fight—"

Deirdre glared, her small, perfect chin defensively out. "We're not going to fight. I just hope he gets sand up his ass."

Then, in an instant, all Dierdre's defensive bravado seemed to collapse. She had glanced across the room to find Evan watching. His look concentrated on her wholly, in a deep, disturbing way.

4

THE THREE-CAR TRAIN to Casablanca waited in the early morning mist. A mob of Arabs thronged the platform, more Arabs than the train could possibly hold. Some murmured farewells to each other, the swirls of their djellabas embracing like clouds as they kissed. Others in a steady stream were boarding the second-class cars. They carried cardboard suitcases, often held together with pieces of string; paper parcels; children and live chickens; bundles of firewood; odd pieces of furniture; loose clothing; more chickens; more children. At the end of the last car a farmer led a goat onto the train.

By contrast, except for the penetrating din from outside, the first-class car was quite sedate. Green plastic and gray leatherette. Folding glass-doors that creaked and often stuck. In fact, only two of the compartments were occupied. In one of them an Italian businessman sat arguing with his heavy blonde German wife. Had she packed his handkerchiefs? Then where were they? Perhaps that thief of a maid in the hotel. The wife mildly inquired what led him to believe that the maid was a thief. It was evident—one had only to look at her. The husband adored these arguments; they filled him with the hope that one day he would be able to arouse his impassive wife to his own furious argumentative pitch.

The other couple, in a compartment several spaces down, consisted of the two American women: Deirdre and Barbara. Both wore the somewhat startled look of people unaccustomed to being up at that hour; in fact Deirdre yawned as though she could easily go right back to sleep, while Barbara looked anxiously wide-awake.

Deirdre's costume was almost as flamboyant as that of the night before: a stiff lace tunic over raspberry silk shirt, above heavy pale green pants, and over all, a green cape. Barbara was more conventionally attired in a gray flannel pants suit.

They were surrounded with expensive pieces of hand luggage: briefcases, cameras, art portfolios, makeup cases, jewelry cases, straw tourist bags. Barbara kept rearranging things, trying for some unobtainable order, while Deirdre watched the scene in the mist outside.

"I wish first-class weren't so empty," Barbara whispered. "I mean really, I feel like the oppressor."

"Mm." Deirdre brought her attention, or at least her gaze, back into the compartment, but she spoke as though continuing an interior monologue. "You know," she said, "there are seven hundred and twenty-three thousand Ron Kesselmans in New York. You can get them at Bloomingdale's. You can even pick the style. Cool. Super cool. God, I'm glad I never married him."

Barbara raised her eyebrows, questioning rather than surprised. She had heard most of this before.

"Well, there is a difference," Dierdre expanded, quite serious.

"Deirdre," Barbara began severely. "I always did think it would be a mistake, your working with Ron again. I mean, who can be civilized sixteen hours a day?"

Deirdre made a wry face, pulling down the corners of her mouth. "When we were living together, Ron and I were very civilized," she said. "In fact, we were exquisite. Do you know that we never sweated in bed?" Her voice had tightened, become high and taut. She knew that she was embarrassing Barbara, but she was demon-driven; she couldn't stop.

"Sweetie—" Barbara protested feebly.

"It's true." Deirdre had almost begun to enjoy the game. "Eleven months and not one drop of sweat. I guess that's the longest I've ever held a pose."

Suddenly an image of Ron and herself as they had been five years ago came to Deirdre: The exquisite couple out on the town, out everywhere in their flamboyant, very "now" clothes: hamburgers at P. J. Clarke's, dancing in a corner at one of Plimpton's parties, having a late snack at Elaine's.

Beautifully photographed. Hard to tell she's pregnant.

And long after midnight the two beautiful people lie marooned on their king-sized bed. She reaches a long way to touch and stroke his perfectly smooth back. She moves closer, still stroking, caressing his flesh.

He turns to her and asks with his own version of sympathy, "Do you feel very sexy tonight?"

She murmurs, "No, of course not," and turns away. To herself she mutters, "You make it sound like some ugly disease."

"What?"

"Nothing."

"Ooh," said Barbara, "you are boiling at him."

"Well for God's sake—we have a child in New York. Ron hasn't seen Marcus in almost two months. Hey, does this train ever move?"

Outside, the jostling, murmurous crowd continued its pantomime. Dierdre watched a young woman with three children clinging to her shirts, very close to each other in size, delivering a mixture of endearments and scoldings to her young husband who was about to board the train. An ancient farmer slowly, laboriously crossed the platform, aided by a gnarled cane and two stalwart young men—his grandsons perhaps. Great-grandsons, Dierdre decided. Camels brayed. A goat began to bleat. And in the distance she heard a drum and a flute playing. The music of Marrakesh.

"Marcus has you," Barbara said. "And your mother."

"Barbara, you know that doesn't quite do it."

Barbara sighed. "I do know."

Deirdre stuck her chin out defiantly. "You know," she said, "I'm going to have to deal with Ron until Marcus is grown."

"Exactly. That's what I *don't* understand. *What* were you trying to prove by working with him?"

Deirdre gave that a little thought. "I wonder. I'm not sure. Masochism? God knows Ron is the masochist's dreamboat."

Barbara's laugh was sad rather than sardonic.

"Or maybe I need him around to prove that my life's always been the other guy's fault," Deirdre went on soberly. "Now wouldn't *that* be a comfy point of view."

Barbara felt the conversation had got out of hand and she recommenced her hopeless task of rearranging luggage. Then a more cheerful thought struck her, and she said, "We'll be in Paris by five, Deirdre. Do you want to have dinner with anyone?"

But Deirdre's attention had been caught by something outside the window. Barbara peered out, but found nothing remarkable. "Deirdre?" she said again.

Deirdre turned back into the compartment. "It's that man," she said. "The young one who was with Fitzgerald last night."

Outside, on the platform, Evan was showing his

ticket to the conductor. He was wearing the clothes that he had the night before, Levis and a brown corduroy coat, and he carried a knapsack.

The conductor gestured toward the first-class car, and Evan hopped on board and began to walk down the corridor. He passed the still-wrangling German-Italian couple and almost went past Deirdre and Barbara. But he stopped to smile and to wave before he disappeared down the corridor.

Deirdre sighed and spoke as much to herself as to Barbara.

"Why don't men look like that any more?"

"Well, he is terribly good-looking."

"I didn't mean that. God—good-looking men!" Deirdre dismissed them all with a gesture of her hand.

"Well—like what?" asked Barbara.

"Like—like something could still be new to them."

Evan had some difficulty in opening the door to his compartment. It stuck; he had to put down his knapsack and use both hands, which he did with considerable impatience. He stalked into the compartment and thrust his knapsack up onto the luggage rack. He slid the door closed and sat down on the banquette, frowning, looking at his watch. He remembered that he had brought nothing new to read and that he had read all the paperbacks in his knapsack many, many times. Irritably he turned to the window, and scowled at the crowd as though those gentle people were delaying the train.

There was a terrible jolt; the whole train shuddered and gasped, and Evan smiled with relief. For the first time he understood that he had been afraid it would never leave.

More relaxed, he began to scrutinize the row of framed advertisements above the opposite banquette. Tourist posters: sunbathers on a Moroccan beach, skiing in the Atlas mountains, water skiers in the Mediterranean. Pretty girls in pretty places, and signs that beckoned: "COME NOW— TRAVEL IS EASIER AND EASIER."

Unaccountably Evan could feel the first cool tentacles of depression creeping into his mind.

The train was moving away from the city, from the terra-cotta walls that glowed even redder in the early morning light; away from the outer ramparts and the range of mountains beyond. The track ran through a palm grove; giant fronds waved and rattled above the lurching train.

Evan tried concentrating on the palms and on the motion of the train, as though they would remove him from the contents of his own mind. But then, the train began to slow down. It jolted and jerked, slowed almost to a halt, only to continue at what Evan felt was an unbearably diminished pace.

He looked out, craning his neck, his face against the glass, but all he could see was palm trees. Then, suddenly, a slowly moving, slowly swaying procession: camels crossing the tracks. A camel market, in fact: hundreds of camels, brought in for sale or barter from the farthest reaches of the desert. Their owners clustered in groups, ragged men, tired and dusty, there to haggle and to socialize.

Evan had stopped looking. His elbows on his knees, he bent his head down and pressed his knuckles hard against his forehead. The depression that was, these days, never very far away had arrived in earnest.

5

IN HER COMPARTMENT Deirdre leafed indifferently through a fashion magazine. Her picture—full face, with rainbows of shadow around her eyes—was on the cover, which this year, today, this morning, as she crossed the grasslands of North Africa, she barely noticed.

At one time she had been ferociously ambitious —dying to come to New York, to be a model, to *make it*. And she sometimes tried to remember that part of herself: the pretty Ohio high-school girl in cautiously cared-for clothes who craved high style, who yearned for a vivid and expensive life. As though she could comfort that girl, could say: yes, you'll get it all. And more.

You'll get a man named Derek who adores you and who is the editor of an important magazine. And who is married.

You'll get a husband named Ron.

And a beautiful son named Marcus.

But today she merely looked at her elegant, stylish image and thought: God, do they really think anyone else will put that stuff on their eyes?

Barbara, with a pencil behind her ear, another in her hand, was looking over a sheet of photo contacts, circling what she liked. "Say, look at this!" and she extended the sheet with the circled picture to Deirdre.

"Terrific," said Deirdre listlessly.

"Thanks a lot." Barbara's irony was light. She was more apt to worry about people than to scold. She worried about her husband, Charlie, and her three daughters, and sometimes she even worried about the fact that she worried. "Mother, don't *worry*," the girls all said, with varying degrees of impatience in their voices. And she often worried about Deirdre, though sometimes chiding herself. "Look, stupid, all you need is one more daughter."

Barbara went on working, but as the train slowed down and lurched to its near-halt, the two women both looked up and then out the window at the procession of camels. Pointing, imagining the smell, Barbara held her nose and Deirdre laughed.

And then they returned to their separate preoccupations. They were, on the whole, two women very affectionately at ease with each other. Deirdre took up her magazine again and Barbara her contact sheets.

The train was crossing the rocky plains north of Marrakesh, beneath an endless pale blue African sky. The rocks were worn and gray, rising out of the wrinkled, desolate land. Deirdre shivered a little, put her magazine down and picked up a French novel from the seat beside her. She began to cut the pages with her nail file. Then, as abruptly as she had begun she stopped, and threw the book aside. She spoke tentatively, "Barbara?"

Barbara looked up.

"I want to ask you something." Deirdre studied her companion and then went on. "Tell me: how often do you and Charlie make love?"

More surprised than shocked by the question, Barbara responded shrewdly: "Doing a little comparison shopping?"

"Maybe." Then, quickly, "You don't have to tell me."

"It's okay. We try to manage every Saturday afternoon, when the girls aren't around. Except of course in football season."

Deirdre laughed. "I didn't know you liked football."

"Hate it. But Charlie does. It's called adjusting, darling."

Barbara thought to herself. Always adjusting—husband-babies-job. Job, not exactly "career," especially in the beginning, when her proofreading had paid the rent and groceries while Charlie was in law school. And always the conflicts: should she quit work and do all the housework herself? Would Charlie and the girls be better off? Were the Swedish *au pairs* really good with children? The Swedish girls came with her rather rapid promotions; the job became a career. But if she didn't work, even with Charlie's increasing success it would be hard to keep up the house at Martha's

Vineyard, not to mention the cherished winter vacations in Jamaica. The children loved the sandy summers, and in Jamaica she and Charlie made love during the long siestas. So Barbara continued with her job, and sometimes she liked it, sometimes not. And Charlie and the children thrived, and Barbara worried.

Deirdre smiled, and Barbara went back to her copy. And Deirdre to nervously doing nothing.

Then, suddenly, Deirdre snatched up her purse and began searching for something in it. Distraught, she pulled out one thing after another: eyebrow brush, compact, Kleenex. "Damn!"

Barbara looked up mildly. "What's wrong?"

"The grass I bought. I must have left it at the hotel."

"Darling, it's eight o'clock in the morning."

"I know. I wonder if that fellow down the way—"

"Is that really such a good idea?" asked Barbara. Then she observed, "Sweetie, you're as jumpy as a catfish."

"I *know*."

Barbara began rewriting her copy, but Deirdre continued to brood about the grass.

After a few minutes Barbara looked up, frowning. "Catfish *do* jump, don't they?"

Evan had begun to feel claustrophobic; he stood up to stretch. But he didn't stretch, he just stood there, lost in his own thoughts. Which suddenly became unbearable. The compartment was a jolting, rattling cage. For escape he turned to the window, and was confronted with an eternity of arid plains—no life, nothing ahead.

In an instant awful tears welled up in his eyes, and he pressed his fist against the window, fighting them off.

The door of his compartment creaked open.

Evan whirled around.

Deirdre was embarrassed when she saw the tears. "Oh—I'm sorry—"

He turned away from her, fighting for control. "You ever hear of knocking?"

"I'm sorry," she said again. A stranger's tears—especially those of this particular stranger—were more than she could handle, or even cared to attempt. It unnerved her to think that the young man she had assumed to be so fresh and untroubled could be so obviously deeply upset. She backed out into the corridor, so that when Evan turned to face her again she was gone.

Impulsively, he followed her as she headed toward her own compartment. Over the noise of the jolting train he called out, "Hey!"

She heard but kept on going.

"No—wait."

Deirdre stopped and reluctantly turned around. They faced each other in the narrow corridor, both bracing themselves with their arms extended, hands pushed against the train sides.

"What did you want?" Evan asked. He felt

suddenly that it was very important for him to know.

"Nothing, really."

But Evan insisted. His blue-eyed gaze was demanding. "What was it?" he asked again.

Instead of answering she found herself saying, "Are you all right?" She hadn't meant to ask that, but she was still shaken by having intruded on his grief.

"Sure, I'm okay. But what did you want?"

"I'm ashamed to say. I shouldn't have bothered you. . . . I thought maybe you had some grass I could buy." She finished lamely and turned away.

"Why shouldn't you bother me?" Evan was determined to deny the fact that she had witnessed his tears of despair.

Deirdre faced him again but couldn't answer him.

He began to smile. "As a matter of fact, I don't have any grass. Never travel with the stuff." He laughed then, and she asked him what he thought was so funny.

"I don't know. I've never been hit on a train before . . . never at eight-thirty in the morning, either."

She sniffed at the air and caught herself as the train lurched sideways. "Somehow I don't seem so funny to me."

Evan sobered instantly. Though her attempt at haughtiness and the jerking train made the picture of Deirdre truly comic, by this time he didn't feel like laughing any more. She was so beautiful —so beautiful and sad and nervous, this American girl in her elegant expensive clothes.

"I can get you some—those Arabs in the other car," he said.

"It doesn't matter. Really," she said.

For a moment they looked at each other, each aware for that moment of the trouble in the other's mind, if not its cause. And just as Evan was about to say something more Deirdre said, "Thanks, anyway," and managed a little smile before she disappeared into her compartment.

Silent, very preoccupied, Deirdre settled herself and took up her book again.

Barbara watched her curiously. After a decent interval she asked, "Where were you?"

"Out of my depth."

"Oh?"

But Deirdre continued to read, or to try to read her bright new French novel, and Barbara resigned herself. Her curiosity was obviously not going to be satisfied at the moment.

6

AFTER DEIRDRE disappeared, Evan stayed on alone in the swaying narrow corridor, not knowing why. He watched the Italian businessman come out of his compartment and head for the lavatory at the end of the car. They exchanged slight smiles of greeting, the Italian's much warmer than Evan's. Evan went quickly back to his compartment. He was afraid that, re-emerging, the Italian would join him, wanting conversation, and at the same time he told himself that he was being ridiculous. "So what?" went the familiar interior monologue. "So we exchange a few banalities on the scenery, at worst on African politics. Will he want the story of my life, any more than I'd want his?" Besides, he didn't want to talk to the Italian. If he wanted to talk to anyone, which was questionable, it would be Deirdre. She was so beautiful he could hardly stand to think about her. He wasn't sure that he could talk to her at all.

Back in his compartment he reached into his knapsack for one of the worn paperbacks. And sat down to read *The Magic Mountain* for perhaps the twentieth time, but Mann had lost his magic on the twentieth round, and Evan couldn't bring himself to continue.

The train passed a herd of sheep, grazing on a hillside. In the distance a tiny hamlet appeared as a dot on the horizon. But it was all so dreary.

Restlessly, he got up and walked down the corridor again. He noticed that Deirdre was not in her compartment. He moved to the end of the car and glanced into the next one—the second-class car. Deirdre had apparently just entered it.

The second-class car was quite another world. No dignified, remote compartments—the whole car was open and dozens of Arabs were packed on too few crude wooden benches; a few sat on the floor or stood against the windows, staring out. Some of them dozed; others were eating breakfasts from paper-wrapped packages. Most of them simply sat there with the infinite endurance of the second-class traveler. A child or two cried; a few chickens flapped noisily about the car. Otherwise, except for the noise of the train, an odd quiet prevailed.

Deirdre stood there, impossibly blonde and smart, wrapped in her long green cape. She was casing the Arab men, seeking a likely prospect for her quest. Everyone stared at her, but mutely, without much real curiosity—she was too distant from the territory of their imaginations. Only the goat was really curious about her; it ambled toward her and sniffed amiably. She gave it a look of mock defiance.

Watching from the other car, Evan smiled to himself.

Deirdre, having made her choice, approached an old man. He was seated somewhat apart from the others on a bench, in a worn djellaba, leaning forward on his cane.

Quietly, in her best new Berlitz French, she said, "Monsieur?"

He looked up.

"Do you—do you have any *kif*?" She said the carefully composed sentence very quickly.

The old man shook his head regretfully. This was clearly an answer rather than a moral comment.

Not knowing quite what to say, she thanked him and began to look further around the car.

A younger Arab, who had been staring at her and listening to the interchange, caught her eye and gave her a flashing smile. Moving a step in his direction, she asked simply *"Kif?"*

No response. Deirdre looked nervously back toward the first-class section, as though for a possible escape route. It seemed to occur to her for the first time that she might be asking for trouble.

But then, as she looked at the younger Arab again, he nodded.

"How much?" she asked.

"Eighty dirhan."

Pleased at the simplicity of the exchange, Deirdre opened her purse to get the money, when another Arab intervened, saying, "Wait, I'll give you a better price."

In French, to Deirdre, the first Arab said, "Don't listen to him." And then he shouted in Arabic, "What is your problem? You mind your own business!"

At that, several other Arabs got up from their benches to join the group around Deirdre. Not menacing: they were much more intent on each other than on her, but Deirdre drew back a little.

In both Arabic and French they began to shout at each other:

"I can do better—"

"Seventy-five dirhan—"

"Over here, mademoiselle—"

"Seventy dirhan—superior quality—"

Deirdre began to quail a little. Her French gave out: in English she said weakly, "Fellows, wait a minute."

Evan began to laugh to himself as he saw what was happening. He was delighted at the diversion, and, in a way, with Deirdre; he decided that she had to be given a lot of credit for sheer guts. How many girls would walk into a car full of Arabs crossing Morocco and try to bargain for grass—and the first thing in the morning? But then he hadn't really known any American girls for quite a while; perhaps the whole breed had changed.

He watched as the tumult around her built, as more men joined the group, and added their voices to the competing shouts. The goat and all the other passengers watched impassively.

"Please—Mademoiselle."

"Fifty dirhan—"

"The finest—"

"Thirty-five."

"Those others are thieves."

Pulling together her French, her small chin thrust out characteristically, Deirdre made a little speech: "Really, it is not the price. The price has nothing to do with it. You don't understand—"

Then she broke off. She looked startled and a little bit afraid. The conductor had just come in from the other second-class car.

He began punching tickets. Swiftly, noiselessly, all the Arabs returned to their seats. Deirdre was left with her original contact, the young Arab, who had not yet seen the conductor. Hurriedly she whispered, "Eighty dirhan?"

He nodded, still oblivious of the conductor.

Deirdre handed him the money.

From the dusty and voluminous folds of his djellaba, he produced an oddly foreign-looking translucent packet; he slipped it to her with a skillfully furtive gesture, and she slipped it into her purse.

"*Merci*."

"*Rien, mademoiselle*."

She turned to leave the car, and found Evan standing there, waiting for her—obviously still very much amused by what he had seen.

Walking slowly toward him, bracing herself against the jolts, Deirdre had to smile too.

The goat followed Deirdre still sniffing in his friendly, casual way.

Evan pointed. "Who's your friend?"

She looked, and laughed aloud. "I don't know," she said. "I believe he thinks he's the social director." Then she asked, "Were you afraid I'd get my throat slit?"

He hesitated. "No, and I don't think you were either, were you?"

She grinned up at him. "No."

"But you did overpay him."

She shrugged. Then she asked, "Are you feeling better now?"

He hesitated, but then decided there was no point in pretending that she had not seen the tears before, "Yes, much better." And he stepped aside as she came back into their car.

7

AFTER THE CROWDS in the second-class car, first-class seemed almost desolate. In his compartment the Italian businessman gently snored, while his wife watched with an unblinking, malevolent eye. Deirdre and Evan walked past them, balancing themselves like passengers on a storm-driven ship. They passed several unoccupied compartments; empty spaces of sand whirled against the windows.

A little mocking, a little defensive, Deirdre asked Evan if he cared to turn on.

He waited a minute. "I don't think so."

"Is that a judgment?"

Looking straight at her he said, "Yes, I guess it is."

Slowly they walked past Deirdre's compartment where Barbara was still absorbed in her work.

"On what grounds?" Deirdre narrowed her eyes.

"Well, for one thing, it's early in the morning."

"So I've been told. You some kind of reality freak?"

He laughed, but she did not; she remained defensive. "It's a long trip, and you can only look at so many sheep."

He gestured toward the grasslands beyond the window panes. "And you're in a country like this every week?"

"I don't see you hanging out the window with a camera."

He sobered a little. "No, you're right." He moved on away from her and pushed at the door of a compartment that was not his.

"You opened the wrong door, too," she said.

"*Touché.*" He took his hand from the door and leaned back against the brass window railing.

Decisively Deirdre opened the door to the empty compartment. Inside, she pulled down the shades, blocking the view from the corridor. But when she had finished she saw that Evan was walking off toward his own compartment. She stepped out into the corridor again. One hand on her hip, she said "Hey."

He paused and turned around.

"Where're you going?" she asked. "I mean— how far by train?"

He hesitated, then said, "Casablanca."

"And then?"

More hesitation. "Paris." Visibly forcing himself to go on, he added, "To catch a plane to New York."

She gave a small triumphant smile. "Then I suspect I'll be seeing you again."

Wary, not understanding, he simply looked at her.

"The plane to Paris," she said.

"Sure." Relief made him grin. "Who knows? You turn on strong enough you may get to Paris ahead of us."

With that as his exit line, he reached firmly for the door of his own compartment.

But at that moment the jolting of the train became much more severe; the jolts were as violent as if they were off the track and out into an open country of rocks. Rounding a curve, the coaches lurched and swayed precariously.

Evan and Deirdre clung to their separate doors.

"Wow, what's this?" he asked.

She laughed.

The shaking continued—was it possible that they were going around in a circle? It got worse. Exhilarated by the ridiculous shaking, in which they could not quite believe, Deirdre and Evan looked at each other and laughed with a sort of childish glee.

Then gradually the train straightened out, and the shaking began to subside.

Deirdre smoothed down her hair, and adjusted her cape, pulling herself together. Feeling Evan's eyes on her, she smiled self-consciously.

Evan looked at her with great seriousness—he seemed to be considering, making a decision. Accustomed to appraisals of quite another sort, Deirdre was discomfited by this one. Evan's regard was purely personal; he wasn't wondering in what light she would photograph best—the right light for what Ron had termed her "difficult" coloring—nor how much toothpaste could be sold with closeups of her teeth.

They were soon distracted from their silent appraisals—the train had subsided to its earlier bumpy progress; in fact it seemed to be slowing to a stop again. Looking out, Deirdre and Evan saw another herd of camels at a little distance from the train.

Deirdre said, "My God, I really think I've had all the camels I can stand in one day."

"I had a kindergarten teacher once who looked like a camel," Evan told her.

"You're kidding."

"Really. Miss McArdle."

They looked at each other, laughing a little.

Evan said, "You know something?"

She gave him a wary look, but he went on.

"I could use some company," he said.

Deirdre, accustomed to a variety of games, was taken aback by his directness. She teased him, "High or straight?"

He answered her seriously. "Couldn't we try for straight?"

8

THE TRAIN APPROACHED a small village of reddish huts of clay, with flat roofs and tiny windows, huts clustered tightly together, as though for protection from the surrounding space.

Evan asked, "Deirdre what?"

"McCluskey."

They were seated on opposite banquettes in his compartment: Deirdre close to her window, Evan more relaxed than she, sprawled in the center of the seat.

"You're kidding," he said. "Deirdre McCluskey?"

She gave a rueful little laugh. "I suppose mother felt the Deirdre would make up for something."

He smiled, but the smile was again too warm, too personal, for Deirdre. In her world everyone played it very, very cool. To warn him, her voice took on an impersonal tone as she recounted: "There was an Irish princess named Deirdre. Deirdre of the Sorrows. According to the legend, when she was born it was prophesied that she'd make a lot of people unhappy." She gave Evan a small sly look.

No reaction.

She went on. "A prince fell in love with her and died because of it."

"What an imagination your mother must have," was Evan's comment. And then he asked, "Do you tell that story to everyone?"

"As a matter of fact, I usually do."

In the village, in the midst of a small dusty square, there was a well and some open tubs where women were scrubbing clothes. On the outskirts of the village, gardens of dusty, stunted plants dotted the area. All the village activity stopped as the train went through, and the villagers looked up from their pursuits: from gathering water and washing clothes, from gardening, and from chasing long-legged chickens and small goats away from the gardens. All those impassive faces regarded the train, not smiling, not reacting to what they saw in any visible way.

Deirdre waved, smiling and looking from face to face, but she might have been a picture—or the cover of a magazine—for all the reaction she inspired.

"Wow," she said. "Talk about coming across."

"Probably good for you."

She made a face at him and laughed.

And then she asked, "Have you been in Morocco long?"

Sobering, he nodded.

She hesitated, but only for a moment. "Why?" she asked. "Are you a student?"

"No."

"Working?"

Now he hesitated, then said, "No, just traveling."

After another pause, during which they simply looked at each other, Deirdre said, "Well, I think I've used all my openers."

He laughed then, as she did. "Okay, I'll try for one. Where're you from?"

"Originally?"

"Well, yes."

"A town in Ohio called Steubenville," she told him.

He laughed. "What do you know. We might have met, even dated. I'm from West Virginia. Fayette."

Somewhat defensively she said, "I haven't been back there for years." Despite herself, Deirdre shuddered slightly as she recalled the house in Steubenville: the yellow, one-story house that needed paint, a sagging porch that needed new supports. An ugly house, a house full of needs.

At that moment a slight tapping sound in the corridor made them both look up. Knocking on their door, smiling slyly, was a fruit vendor: a very small man, his djellaba wrapped around him, his head encased in a gaudy, and very dirty, turban. He spoke to Evan in French: "Lovely fruit? Fresh—very fresh fruit?"

In Arabic Evan said, "Good, I'll take those two and those."

"Fifty dirhan."

"No, I'll give you thirty."

"Sir—forty—"

Evan took the fruit, placed it on the seat beside him, and counted out money.

Smiling and bowing, the vendor went back out into the corridor, closing the door behind him with a mighty creak.

Evan took out a pocket knife and began to peel the fruit. He was exceptionally deft, sure and quick with his hands. Deirdre watched; at first her gaze stayed on his expert hands, but after a moment she began instead to watch his face.

Unaware of her stare, Evan asked conversationally, "Where's your family? Still there?"

"My mother lives with me in New York."

"Your father dead?"

"I don't know." She waited, then said, "He took off when I was thirteen."

He gave her a level look. "That must have been a little rough."

She shrugged, to minimize it, but her voice got a little high as she went on. "He got tired of something. The coal mine. Or Steubenville. Or mother." She paused, and looked out the window for a moment. "I used to think he'd gotten tired of me," she said.

"Where's your father, Deirdre? I haven't seen him around for a while." The kindly neighbor.

"Oh, he's gone out to California. When he's settled he's going to send for us."

"Oh, I see. Well, that's nice."

Did anyone believe her, or was she only talking to herself?

But not even postcards came, not from California, nor anywhere else. He might never have lived in Steubenville, nor had a daughter whom he called his beauty.

Instead of interrupting her reverie, Evan handed her a piece of peeled fruit—and waited for a reaction as she bit into the pulp, with her shining, perfect teeth.

"Well?" he asked.

She took another bite. "It's so *cool*," she said, "What is it?"

"Cactus fruit."

He started to peel another fruit, then stopped and asked, "You think your friend might be hungry?"

"Barbara? Always hungry. You can give her a try," said Deirdre—pleased with him for his thoughtfulness.

"Who is she, anyway?"

"Her name's Barbara Newman. She's a fashion editor."

"What's a fashion editor?"

She frowned, as though the phrase were self-explanatory. "What do you mean?"

"Well, what does she do?"

"She worries a lot."

Evan laughed and got up, carrying the half-peeled fruit. Outside Barbara's compartment he rapped on the glass and held up the cactus for her to see. She smiled, delighted, and pantomimed hunger with a clutching gesture at her stomach. So he opened the door and handed her the fruit.

"Oh—you've come to save my life! Thank you—thank you," she said.

"Aim to please," he drawled, mock-Southern. Then he smiled and was gone.

Barbara's glance followed him out, a glance that was lingering and speculative. Among other things, she had the curious notion that Evan and Deirdre looked somewhat alike.

9

EATING THEIR FRUIT, Evan and Deirdre were again settled opposite each other. Outside the sun warmed the stretches of sand and rock, and the colors changed from gray to brown.

Very carefully casual, Evan asked, "Who was the guy last night?"

She looked up, and he added, "The one in the restaurant."

She gave it a little thought but answered only, "He's a photographer." She recrossed long legs, still considering, weighing, choosing words. But then she burst out, "Of course he's a bloody genius."

He laughed, then asked seriously, "But to you? He's a photographer?"

It would have been easy enough to say yes, to leave it more or less at that, and Deirdre considered the possibility of that half-lie. For one thing she was so tired of talking about Ron and of thinking about him. She had talked for years to her friends, to Barbara and others, had talked briefly to a psychiatrist, and no one had ever come up with an explanation: why Ron for Deirdre, why Ron as the father of her child.

Evan was still looking at her, and quickly she said, "No, he's a little more than that: he and I have a son." And she waited for his next question.

It was simpler than she had expected.

"You divorced?"

"We were never married."

No reaction to that.

What was terrible—was even crazy—was that Deirdre realized she had no really good memories of Ron. Moments of intensity, even of occasional passion, but no real tenderness. No long smooth happy days. Each day contained small or sometimes large-scale bitterness, often over nothing: where to go for dinner, whose cleaning bill had been highest, which of them had paid for the last party's booze. At times Deirdre had an obscure sense that Ron was jealous of her—that he felt that he, rather then she, was the beautiful person who deserved to be photographed. His self-absorption made her feel unattractive, and she tried harder and harder to please him, to be more and more beautiful, to learn to cook and to be a graceful hostess—finally to have a perfect handsome son for him. And each effort, up to and including the last, the birth of Marcus, brought on a harder put-down.

Evan asked, "Are you two still—whatever you were?"

Distractedly she answered. "No. Not for a long time."

His questions had a quality entirely new to her, something she couldn't quite define. She felt his interest and clearly his friendliness, but beyond that there was an urgency about him. He came on like a man without much time. But at his age? She was deeply puzzled and intrigued.

"Tell me about your little boy," said Evan.

She brightened at that. "His name is Marcus," she told him. "He's four and a half." How to describe anyone as close and loved as Marcus was: his light hair, dumb jokes? His sleepy clean smell when he was ready for bed? She gave it up. "I'm sure he's going to be president," she said. "And, of course, I'll be first lady."

"How does Ron feel about Marcus?"

She made a sour face. "Not exactly enthusiastic."

"Why do we have a nurse if you can't go out and leave the kid?"

"We were out last night and three nights last week—"

"Well, Mother D., I can't really say that you're a lot of fun—"

A week later they separated. Deirdre found a new East Seventies place, and her mother came to live with her—with her and Marcus—

The train was passing grassland, bright green in the high midmorning sunshine. There was an abandoned fortress of crumbling gray stone; it could have been from any age at all, from any war. Also timeless were the shepherd and his flocks that appeared just then, crossing the grass.

"What about your family?" Deirdre asked.

Evan looked momentarily sad. "My father's a judge, he's—"

"In West Virginia?"

He nodded.

"I was right," she said. "Our paths would never have crossed."

"You sure about that?"

"Come on, the coal miner's daughter and the judge's son? Sounds like a bad novel. Boys like you came to my part of town for one nasty reason."

"I might have been different." His tone was much lighter than hers had been, but his eyes were serious.

Brightly she asked, "Do you have brothers or sisters?"

"Three sisters."

Deirdre had a jealous vision of those three favored girls, the daughters of the judge, soft-spoken and easily graceful, probably graduating from places like Vassar and Sarah Lawrence, marrying Princeton and Yale. No Rons for them.

"Christ, D."—Ron had rarely used her name—"can't you get the coal mines out of your voice? Your sentences with all those *r*'s sound like obstacle courses. I mean you don't actually have to advertise that disadvantaged background of yours, do you now?" And so: voice lessons from Mrs. Fitzgibbons, who smoothed and softened and rendered neutral what had been harsh but personal, until, sometimes, listening to herself as she talked, Deirdre felt that she was hearing a recording of someone else's voice.

Smiling, remembering his sisters, Evan said, "of course they all spoiled me rotten."

"Of course."

"Actually we all spoiled each other. It was really nice."

"Was? What happened?"

He frowned, and waited a minute before he said, "Nothing, really." Shrugged. "You grow up."

She looked at him curiously, but let it go. Well, why not? She wasn't especially anxious to discuss her family either. Almost formally, in her well-trained voice she asked, "How long have you been traveling?"

"Quite a while."

This so-obvious evasion made them look at each other and laugh.

And then Deirdre said, "All right. No more questions."

The train pulled to an unexpected grinding halt.

10

OUTSIDE THE MOTIONLESS locomotive, the engineer and the brakeman were standing by the engine, studying the machinery. The conductor stood watching them. All three men looked at the same time serious, passive and unhurried. Something of the sort happened every day. Arab passengers swarmed out of their two cars to move about and to look. Several joined the engineer and the brakeman at the head of the train; they looked, poked, offered advice. The goat munched peacefully on a bush.

Some distance from the train a gentle hill rose up from the grasslands, up to a small walled village. An irregularly beaten path led up to the wall and a gate. In the heavy sunshine, Deirdre, Barbara, and Evan strolled toward the gate.

Barbara looked anxiously back at the train. "Are you *sure* they won't start without us?"

Evan had been the one to deal with the conductor, and now he tried to reassure her. "They said they wouldn't."

"Where's your sense of adventure?" Deirdre teased.

"You may feel that missing a train in this place is an adventure, but I'm too old for that kind of fun."

Deirdre laughed. "But marooned in Morocco? Think of the possibilities." She seemed possessed by some private excitement. Almost as though she were high she laughed again. "We might come across the parched body of Ron," she said, "chewed by buzzards. Are there buzzards?"

Evan was preoccupied, and he too glanced back at the train.

"Do you think that there's a chance this place has a john?" asked Barbara.

Deirdre laughed at her. "Why didn't you use the one on the train?"

"I was afraid."

"What makes you think you'll have any better luck here?" asked Deirdre. "For a realistic lady—"

The village could have been deserted. Primitive, grass-thatched clay houses, camels dozing in the streets. One old woman appeared: wrinkled, toothless, she stood in one of the dark doorways to stare at the trio of strangers.

"What do they *do* here?" Barbara looked about uneasily. It was too foreign, too remote, for her city girl's imagination.

"They're shepherds," Evan told her. He had formed an affection for this land that he was leaving—probably forever.

"This is where the sheep come home at night." Deirdre echoed Evan's tone. She had unconsciously caught some of his feeling for the place.

Uncharmed, Barbara looked around and found nothing to see. "I suppose it's all very timeless," she said.

They walked along the dusty street, Evan and Deirdre slightly ahead, Barbara lagging behind.

Then they turned a corner, and Deirdre began to smile as teasingly she sang out to Barbara, "Bar-ba-ra-I think it's marketday."

"Ah—treasures—I knew there must be *some-*thing."

There ahead of them in the village square was a tiny market, half a dozen open stalls, where a couple of dozen villagers had gathered to buy and to socialize: squirming children and tired mothers, sun-darkened men. No one looked young, in the sense that Deirdre and Evan were young. Looking at the women in particular, Deirdre felt the impossible distance separating her from them. An impossible difference in their ideas of womanhood: her relative freedom of choice, their almost total lack of it.

"*Tchachkes,*" Barbara said, as though performing an incantation. "I can feel them in the air."

Evan whispered, "What's a *tchachkes?*"

"I'm not sure," Deirdre whispered back. "You might say it's anything that fills an empty space."

Barbara already had begun to search among the wares in the ironmonger's stall. She was looking for an *object,* any object, really, but there were none; there were only crude farm and kitchen implements. Rather desperately Barbara examined a hand trowel—the smallest thing there, but still—so crude and heavy. Too heavy for her suitcase and completely out of place on her Gramercy Park coffee table.

The ironmonger, who was probably about Barbara's age, but who looked at least twenty years older, came over to examine her with the most absolutely impersonal scrutiny she had ever experienced. Up and down he looked at her, in a way that had nothing to do with sex—he may not even have been sure that she was a woman; she was more on the order of an apparition. Uncomfortably Barbara moved away to a weaver's stall where Deirdre was examining small djellabas.

"I'm sure this would be his size." She held out the garment to Evan, as though he would know the right size for Marcus.

Evan smiled.

She turned back to the weaver and nodded and opened her purse.

"I'll do it," Evan told her, and he made the bargain in Arabic with the weaver. She paid and accepted the djellaba, which he had first wrapped in a piece of newspaper.

They went on to the fruit stall: bushel baskets gleaming with lemons, oranges, figs, and cactus fruit, surrounded by an enormous multicolor variety of species. Every spice, every color and scent.

"God, how marvelous!" Deirdre plunged her hands into a huge straw tray.

Evan laughed at her delight. "Myrh or frank-incense?" he asked.

She let the spice spill back into the basket, slowly, over her arms. Then she raised the back of her hand for Evan to sniff.

Using a parody of the old rough voice that Ron had had polished away, she said, "Knock you dead, kid?"

Evan held the look long enough for her to squirm self-consciously, forcing her to look away and to pull at her hand. He sniffed at the fragrance then and nodded, but as though he had forgotten what it was all about.

Deirdre went back to the weaver's stand, where Barbara was relentlessly examining blankets, throw rugs, shawls—all the brilliant harsh wools, the violent strange colors that would never do in her house.

In a mockingly stilted voice Deirdre began: "Yes, I found it in this little village. I think it was called Sidi-El-Boum."

"Stop it, Deirdre. Nobody likes a wise-ass." She didn't bother to look up.

Deirdre and Evan smiled at each other and at Barbara's determined and quite hopeless quest.

When Barbara did look up they were gone. She looked all around the market—they were not there. She shrugged and went on examining the weaver's goods, while the somewhat dazed weaver, from his corner, continued to examine her.

11

AT THE EDGE of the square a small street that led away from the market and the crowd seemed to promise privacy. Faced with that promise, Deirdre and Evan looked at each other for a minute, aware of an excitement that had grown between them, but also reluctant and afraid. Did they really want to be alone?

Deciding, Deirdre started into the narrow street. Evan hesitated for perhaps a moment before following her. Her small American heels made no sound nor hardly any trace in the heavy African dust. He caught up with her and they walked on, open to any destination that might offer itself.

What came to them, around a bend, was another street, at the end of which was a small square thatch-roofed house with a walled garden next to it. The gate to the garden was half-open.

Delighted, Deirdre whispered, "Shall we?"

She started down the street, toward the garden, but then she realized that Evan wasn't coming. She turned and looked at him, her look a question.

He waited, considering, and then came up to her and they moved down the street toward the open gate—both a little breathless, not looking at each other.

The garden was parched and scrubby. Bare hollowed patches and a mild distinctive odor suggested that it was a haven for animals, as well as for people. Now it was deserted, however, a silence emanated from the house: no one home at market time.

Deirdre crossed to the far wall, where, looking over, she could see the train in the distance, the Arab passengers still milling along the tracks.

Evan came to stand near her, but not very near. Together they stood in the unreal silence. Aware of his pulsing blood, Evan fought the need to reach out to her, feel her in his arms. . . .

Then, looking at him fully, Deirdre said, "Do you know what I'd like you to do?"

Silently he returned her look.

She went on. "I'd like you to touch me."

A pause. "I know," he said.

"Well then?"

"I—I don't think so." Very gentle, but clear.

She moved back a little, managing not to wince and making a considerable effort at control. "Well, no one could accuse you of beating around the bush."

He was very serious. "I don't want to—to kill time with you, Deirdre." He gave her name a lilting sound.

Barely controlled, she managed to play it lightly. "I'd never know," she said.

"I would."

"You're very ethical," she mocked, "or maybe you're just a tease."

"Look, don't bait me." He suddenly sounded very tired.

"You were awfully winning on the train, Mr. Bonner," she said.

"You're hard to ignore," he told her flatly.

"Oh, thank you very much indeed." A rising fury sounded now in her voice—in the heat, in the airless garden where nothing grew. But it was easier to be angry than to feel whatever else she had come so close to feeling for him.

He made a small gesture of coming toward her, but she moved back. He stopped. "Look, I—"

Not to be conciliated, Deirdre said, "You know, all I said was *touch*. It was a very simple request." There were splinters of ice in her voice.

He looked at her. Hard. "I'd go right out of my skin. Touching you. And I can't afford that."

"You?" she mocked. "You go out of your skin?" But she knew what he meant; her own skin shivered in response.

"*Don't bait me*." Now it was his blue eyes that were hard and furious.

She turned away—one hand rose but did not quite touch her mouth. Then she turned back to him, and said simply, "You know, this is the second time this morning that you've made me feel ridiculous."

He spoke gently. "You don't have anything to feel ridiculous about."

"You bet your ass I don't," she blazed. Not looking at him, she began to pick her way across the desiccated garden. And without turning around, "I just want you to know something: I've been thrown out of a lot better places than this."

He smiled, but sadly, with a kind of regret that looked out of place on such a young man.

Gingerly Deirdre sat down on an overturned wheelbarrow, near the wall. Crossing her legs, she held her purse on one knee and pulled it open. She began to search through it.

Evan watched for a moment, then he stared around at the dying, deserted garden, the small space that enclosed them, that made for the moment a tiny and unlikely world for them. As he looked at the half-open gate, he saw an old, gaunt dog approaching from the street; it sniffed at the air and decided against coming in. It went on down the street briskly, as though it had just remembered an appointment. Remembering certain appointments of his own, Evan sighed a little, and then he spoke to Deirdre, "Do you want to go back to the market?"

Instead of answering she turned away from him, so that when he spoke again it was directed at her upturned profile. Evan observed the delicacy of her features, their poignancy, but he merely asked again, "Do you want to go back?"

She faced him squarely. "What's the problem?"

she asked. From her tight breathless voice, it was quite clear which problem she meant.

"About going out of my skin?" He injected a minor note of irony into that.

"If you have to put it that way."

"I know I'd want to stick around," he told her simply. "And I can't do that."

She frowned. "Why not?"

He spread his hands, regarding them help-lessly. "I can't, that's all."

The frown became a scowl. "Man of mystery. Big *bore*."

She resumed the search of her purse, then brought out the packet of grass and some ciga-rette papers. She began to spread out a little grass on the knees of her pale green pants.

Evan came a few steps nearer. "You really need a lot of diversion, don't you?"

"Why don't you go—" she changed her mind with a small grin, and nodded toward the village —"go study the natives."

Somewhat clumsily she pulled out two papers, licked an edge and began to push some grass into the fold. It was ground very fine and some spilled out. She plucked at it, gave up, and brushed it off.

Evan asked, "Can I tell you something?"

"What?"

"We have touched," he said.

Holding the unfinished joint on her lap, she said, "Okay, I lost my head." She looked at him very directly. "It's been a long time since I've seen a man cry." The last man who cried before her was Derek, when he decided, after all, not to leave his wife, but finally Derek's tears were no more real than anything else about him: his perfect gray hair, his words of love.

Then, back into her old defiant tone, she said, "And, as you've just pointed out, I collect unique experiences."

When he spoke it was oddly affectionate. "You give with one hand, you try your damnedest to take it away with the other, don't you?"

"You're all words, Charlie Brown." But she smiled as she said it. And rolling the joint into shape, licking it again, she got up. "I think I'd like to get out of here," she said.

They looked at each other for a long minute. Then Evan tore his look away. With a violent gesture—pushing with both hands, as though pushing the future away—he turned and opened the gate, and they left their unenchanted garden.

Deirdre started off in the direction from which they had come, but Evan pointed the other way. "This is probably quicker," he said.

In a depressed silence they walked along in the direction he had chosen. Groups of villagers, coming home from the market passed Deirdre and Evan and backed against the wall to stare at the fair Americans, but Deirdre and Evan did not look around or even seem to notice. Ahead of them was the market, now slowly losing its small population.

In a small voice, Deirdre asked, "You don't have a match, do you?"

He shook his head.

"You have any vices left?" She was almost querulous.

He shook his head again, just glancing over in her direction.

She stopped, and shuffling through her purse, came out with a box of matches. But as she started to light the joint, with a flicker of a gesture Evan stopped her—a small tap on her hand.

He asked. "Is this your way of saying good-bye?"

She looked at him—petulant, defiant, "I'd like the morning to amount to *some*thing," she said.

"Then *say* good-bye. That would be something."

She struck a pose, defensively playing the model: one knee bent, that leg thrust out ahead, one elbow out, her hand on her hip. She said, "You know, I really object to the way you get to me. I mean, I think you ought to decide where you stand."

"I know where I stand." He looked hard at her. "I know I'd like to do a lot of things that would be stupid."

She returned his look, and her posture softened: angles drawn in, arms passive. Again, the moment was there; it was ready to explode.

But it did not. Nothing happened.

Deirdre said, "Oh Christ." She dropped the joint on the ground and kicked at it with her foot. "The morning's half-over anyway," she said.

She put the packet back, then said "Oh Christ"

again, and took out the *kif*. "What am I going to do with this? I expected to be clean by Casablanca."

Evan took the packet and looked around at a barren space that offered no hiding places, not even a bush or a clump of grass. Then, with a grin and a long windup, he lobbed the packet into the marketplace.

Deirdre began to smile. "Look," she cried out. "There's Barbara."

12

LIKE AN ANCIENT animal that slowly awakened, with jolts and creaks and grunts the train began shaking itself before getting into motion. The Arabs pushed and jostled against each other as the last of them boarded the second-class car. From first-class, the Italian stood beside his wife gesturing to Deirdre, Evan, and Barbara—Barbara laden with not one but two blankets from the weaver's stall—who were hurrying to board.

"*Attention—vitesse*—carry on," the Italian shouted—unsure of their nationality but eager to be of help.

"What matter?" asked his wife. "So—they miss the train."

Evan took Barbara's blankets from her and the three of them began to run. They ran easily, much faster than the laborious pace of the still-recovering train.

But then Barbara lurched to one side—her heel caught in a rut. She cried out "Oh *no!*" And saw that the heel had broken off. "I've got to get to the john," she cried.

She took off her shoe and at the same time Deirdre swept down and collected the heel. The three of them continued their now somewhat lopsided run for the train. Which they reached and just managed to board—all laughing and out of breath.

Inside, in the corridor, Barbara limped hurriedly toward the lavatory, while Evan and Deirdre went into her compartment and took up their positions on opposite banquettes, still gasping a little.

"I'll take the heel," Evan said.

She handed it to him.

"How're you fixed for hammers?"

She reached for her makeup case, a large tomato-red patent-leather box; opening it, she began to look around. At last she handed him a small wooden-handled hairbrush.

"Is that the best you can do?"

She nodded.

Dexterously, Evan made a hammer of the brush and worked at repairing the shoe.

Deirdre watched, admiring his swift and expert hands. Her look went up to his face, and stayed until he glanced up, and their eyes met and held. She was the first to look away, to look out at the endlessly dry scenery—scenery for which she now felt a curious and premature nostalgia.

Barbara came in at that moment, still limping, and fell into the seat next to Deirdre. Feeling something in the air that made her uneasy, she seized on the shoe proffered to her.

She put it on and then stepped down, twisting and turning, making a great show of testing the repair. "Oh, you're a genius," she cried, and then, looking back and forth between Deirdre and Evan, she repeated, somewhat less certainly, "You're an absolute genius."

No one helped her out, and she stumbled on, conversationally shoeless, so to speak, tripping over her good intentions.

"I don't know how we'd have gotten through this trip without you," she said to Evan. "I mean, the fruit and everything."

He smiled at her and then glanced at Deirdre, who was looking out the window.

"Well," Barbara assumed a busy, bustling manner—her usual escape from any such ambiguously charged situation. "I'd better get back to work."

Evan asked her, "You like what you do?"

She grinned. "I like the money."

Evan replayed that bit of dialogue to himself: Who? where? And then remembered: of course, Fitzgerald—Fitzgerald giving the same answer to the same question, and with a little of Barbara's apologetic-defiant smile. And Evan wondered, not for the first time: Isn't there some other way to work or to think about work? As a little boy he had wanted to be a carpenter, and then, as an adolescent, he had had doctor fantasies—and then —then suddenly his choices seemed very diminished.

"And oddly enough I like the people," Barbara went on. "I feel out of place not surrounded by nuts," and she looked fondly at Deirdre.

"I must work!" said Barbara, and this time she pulled out her portfolio, opened it, and brought out her papers.

"Care for a game of gin?" Evan asked Deirdre.

"Sure—for what?"

"For nothing—okay? *Pour le sport.*"

She gave him a wry smile. "*Pour le sport*—okay, you're on."

He put the deck on an opened suitcase between them, and they began a most unspectacular game of gin.

After a while he asked, "You want to take a walk?"

"No, I don't think so." Then, not quite bitterly, she added, "I've had my excursion for the day, I think."

They regarded each other—the moment was heavy.

She looked down at her cards. "Oh. Gin," she said.

More time went by—but less time than it seemed to those two playing a game neither of them wanted to play.

"If you want to stretch?" Deirdre asked.

He said no, that he was fine.

Outside, the scenery was slowly changing. Small whitewashed stone houses lined the tracks; on the narrow dusty streets there were men and women who walked more briskly than the desert villagers and who did not pause to look up at the train—they had seen a lot of trains.

"For Christ's sake," Deirdre said. "We must be coming into Casablanca."

"I can't believe it," said Barbara, beginning to stuff papers back into her portfolio.

Deirdre looked at Evan. "You know, Casablanca, the fabled, mysterious city of romance?"

13

"THIS HAS GOT to be the most unplanned town I've ever seen," remarked Barbara, as she observed the deplorable shacks that alternated with the tall office buildings.

"It looks like the army built it," Evan said grimly.

Deirdre noted the tone of his voice; it imparted more than the remark seemed to require, and she was about to question it when they pulled into the station.

Very conventional French Colonial and very dirty, Deirdre thought distractedly as she forgot her concern with Evan's mood for the moment.

The train had not quite come to a halt when the Arab passengers began to pour out of it; once again it seemed impossible to Deirdre that these two cars could have contained so many people. On the platform they were met by another crowd who waited there, and as at the station in Marrakesh four hours earlier, she heard the gentle murmurs among the billowing djellabas—the sounds of excited reunions mingled with the sonorous partings.

The goat pranced along, sniffing at the unfamiliar air.

The German wife stepped heavily out of the first-class car, followed by her husband, who was signaling for a porter and combing his hair at the same time.

Most of the Arabs were out of their car when the three Americans emerged, following a porter Evan had succeeded in snaring. The porter had stacked most of their luggage onto his cart, but still the three of them were heavily burdened.

Barbara continued awkwardly to try to rearrange the packages in her arms: her portfolio, makeup case, canvas and straw tourist bags. "Just once," she said rather breathlessly, "just once I'd like to arrive somewhere *grace*fully." She turned to Evan, who was carrying her rugs, along with his knapsack. "I think it's marvelous that you can travel with that one little—one little—" but she couldn't find the word for knapsack. "I suppose it's different with men," she finished vaguely.

Deirdre gave a little hysterical laugh and pulled her toward the station. The porter darted ahead with most of their possessions; as though he wanted to escape them, he rose to the challenge of maneuvering through the crowd.

Following as quickly as they could, they almost kept up, then lost him. "How will we know him?" Barbara whispered nervously to Deirdre. "I hate to say this, but they do all look sort of alike."

"He'll be the one with our luggage," Evan told her.

And there, in front of the station, stood the porter, smiling in triumph beside the embarrassing mountain of their luggage.

They all thrust money upon him, with that eager gesture of Americans leaving a country and wanting to divest themselves of what was now meaningless paper.

In Arabic Evan summoned a taxi, and he and the porter loaded on the luggage, as Deirdre and Barbara watched.

"I'm starving," Barbara said. "I suppose we can eat at the airport?"

"What time is the plane?"

"Two o'clock." Barbara looked at her watch. "Oh Lord." She nodded toward the driver. "Does he know the way?" Then, with a second thought, "Well, of course he must—he lives here."

The two women got into the taxi, as Evan and the porter finished with the luggage.

They rode through sparse traffic, through alleys full of bicycles and pedestrians and motorbikes, through the business district of Casablanca where modern white office buildings loomed next to squalid one-story huts. An ancient Arab on a rattling bicycle darted among the cars and busses and violent motorbikes.

Diffidently, Barbara asked Evan, "Do you think —think you might get him to go a little faster?"

Evan spoke to the driver, and the taxi did, indeed, pick up some speed.

Barbara complimented Evan on his Arabic. "It's really impressive."

He paused. "I just know a few words."

"I couldn't learn it in a million years."

No response.

Beyond their speeding windows the city began to thin out: fewer houses, more gardens, dusty streets on which an occasional farm animal appeared: the inevitable chickens and goats. And then they were out in real farmlands: terraced hills, spaced trees.

Compulsively, because she felt silences were somehow unnatural, Barbara asked Evan if he had seen a lot of Morocco.

Another pause. "Not really—mostly Marrakesh."

Barbara gave up—for the moment.

The land about them became desolate—empty, nothing but flat land.

"Maybe there *isn't* any airport," Deirdre teased.

"We landed at one when we came in." Barbara was serious.

"That must have been a mirage."

Then suddenly, sitting like a mushroom in the middle of nowhere, there was the airport: white and squat and unlikely.

Evan and the driver attempted to cope with the luggage, while Deirdre and Barbara, laden with their hand luggage, hurried into the terminal building.

"I'm sure they'll serve something to eat on the plane," Deirdre tried to reassure her friend.

"Promises, promises—"

Followed by a porter, Evan came toward them.

"Do *you* think they'll serve anything on the plane?" Barbara asked him.

"What? Oh sure." Evan seemed distracted.

At the check-in counter Barbara went first. She finished with her business there, and hurried across the lobby, clutching her things and glancing at her watch, headed for customs and immigration.

Dierdre and Evan were assumed by the men behind the desk to be traveling together; his knapsack and her luggage were thrown into one pile. They looked at each other and shrugged. Oh well.

In Arabic a voice blared out over the speaker. Evan strained to understand.

"What is it?"

"I'm not sure."

Then, in French: "Air France Flight 2006 to Paris has been delayed."

"Oh-oh," Deirdre moaned.

The voice, in French, continued. "The new departure time will be announced shortly."

And, just as Barbara was looking around for her companions, the announcer repeated in English: "Air France Flight 2006 flight to Paris has been delayed. The new departure time will be announced shortly."

As Deirdre and Evan came up to her, Barbara exclaimed, "That's us!"

Deirdre laughed. "Looks like you'll have time for lunch after all."

"And after the way I *flogged* that driver."

Not listening to them, nor looking at them,

Evan's troubled gaze was directed at the desks marked in three languages: Customs and Immigration. He frowned and then seemed to brace himself.

14

A GROUP OF arriving passengers, mostly Arab, were clustered at the customs desk. Deirdre and Evan and Barbara squeezed past them and continued on to one of the immigration desks.

At the other, the Italian businessman and his wife stood, elaborately arguing in several languages other than Arabic, with a stone-faced official. The wife, curiously, seemed to side with the official—whatever the problem, clearly she felt it was all her husband's fault.

At their desk, Deirdre and Barbara fumbled through their bags; finally passports were produced and handed to one of the clerks.

Unsmilingly Evan watched the process.

The clerk looked through the women's passports at great length; he read every page, even the blank ones, before finally stamping and handing them back.

Then he turned to Evan. "And your passport, monsieur?"

Reluctantly Evan handed him a folded document, an expression of puzzlement settled on the clerk's face, as he looked from the document to Evan and back.

Then he began to examine it; at excruciating length he looked it over, back and forth. At the end of the performance he handed it to another clerk.

Throughout all this Evan had avoided a backward glance at Deirdre and Barbara, but now he turned to them. "Look, why don't you go sit down?"

Deirdre gave him a long and serious look, and then she and Barbara turned and started over to the waiting room.

Behind them, Deirdre heard a third clerk address Evan in French, "M. Bonner, if you would please come with me?"

Turning around, Deirdre watched as Evan followed the new clerk into a glass-walled office.

"Deirdre—" Barbara pulled lightly at her arm.

Deirdre was still watching. "Wait a minute," she said.

"Deirdre—Deirdre, he could be *anything.*" Barbara frowned with concern for her friend.

"I suppose. But who couldn't?" Deirdre was a little glum.

Inside the office, the clerk handed Evan's document to a uniformed official, clearly of high rank, seated behind the desk. He examined it silently.

Restless, Evan looked out through the glass and watched as Deirdre and Barbara headed toward the waiting area.

The official went on reading, examining.

Evan fidgeted, then—finally—asked, "Didn't Mr. Fitzgerald talk to you? From the embassy?"

No answer, as the man continued to study. His skin was yellowish, very light for an Arab, and wrinkled. Evan briefly fantasized that when the official was an old man his skin would turn to parchment—itself a document.

Finally—"We have to be very certain about these things," the Grand Inquisitor said.

He stamped the document and gave it back to Evan. "I am sorry for the delay." He was formally polite but disapproving.

"So am I," Evan responded, not bothering to conceal a bitter smile.

The waiting room was small and spartan: a few hard benches, a single refreshment stand, one news counter. Arabs stood about in clusters, looking patient. Some Europeans, mainly English, sat along the benches, among the older Arabs and a couple of women with small children. At the newsstand Deirdre was trying to buy some magazines; she struggled with the money and her packages and then with the magazines: American, six months old.

Deirdre took her magazines over to a partially empty bench, and after a minute or two Barbara joined her there. She had managed to buy a sandwich at the refreshment stand and was now trying to unwrap it with one hand.

"You want something? Have a bite of this?"

Barbara coaxed in her best motherly manner.

"No—no thanks."

"God, no wonder you stay so thin."

Instinctively looking up in the direction of the glass office, Deirdre saw Evan emerge. Despite the milling crowds, he spotted them instantly and began to walk over to where they were sitting. With a faint smile he sat down beside them—almost, but not quite as though nothing had happened.

The silence was broken by Barbara, as usual. In her most social voice, she said, "Do you *believe* the red tape in these countries? I suppose everybody just has their little job to do."

Deirdre and Evan exchanged a look that contained affection for Barbara—and her misguided efforts.

Barbara asked Evan if she could get him anything as she headed back to the snack bar.

He smiled. "No thanks."

Deirdre opened one of her magazines, and she looked as though she were reading. But then, after a moment, she turned the magazine upside down, and continued her perusal.

"You get more out of it that way?" Evan asked her.

"Not especially. I'm just showing you how cool and discreet I am."

He sighed sadly. "Look, I'm just a guy you met on a train."

She looked at him. "Oh? Isn't that backstepping a bit?"

No answer.

She sat up straighter and tightened her grip on the magazine, in a parody of fierce concentration —on the magazine that was still upside down.

"Deirdre—"

She made a melodramatic whisper. "Did you kill someone?"

"No."

Her laugh was wry. "Well, it's certainly not a morals charge."

Looking full at her, Evan had almost begun to speak when a fat businessman, in heavy, inappropriate tweeds planted himself in front of them. In German he asked, "May I sit down—please?"

They looked up at him in total incomprehension; he might have been plunked down before them from out of the sky.

He gestured, and at last they understood, they moved to make room for him, and he sat down.

Fanning himself, still speaking in German, he said, "I thank you. This heat is intolerable." He took out a handkerchief and mopped his brow conspicuously.

"I'm a deserter," Evan said, to Deirdre.

"A what?"

"A deserter. From the army."

She responded as if he were speaking another language or explaining calculus. "What are you talking about?"

"I was in Vietnam. I deserted."

"What—" But it was less a question than a small

sound of pain, as though already she almost knew all that would follow.

"Deirdre, could I borrow one of those magazines?" Barbara returned, another sandwich in hand.

Blindly Deirdre stared up at her friend, but she couldn't focus. After an instant she came to and thrust the pile of magazines at Barbara.

"Oh, one's fine."

"Take them!" Deirdre cried out.

Concerned and completely mystified, Barbara studied Deirdre for a moment, then Evan. Smiling uncertainly, she still hesitated. "Well," she said, "I'll see you. Thanks." And with the pile of magazines that she hadn't wanted she made her way to another bench. Once she turned back to look at Deirdre and Evan, who were not looking at her. Then she picked up her sandwich again and began idly to leaf through a magazine whose fashion coverage she had edited a year ago.

Deirdre whispered fiercely, "What are you *talking* about? You were in Marrakesh—"

He was patient, if tired. "Look, it's a long story. I—I've turned myself in."

Fighting this unwelcome news, she spoke angrily. "What do you mean, you've turned yourself in? You're sitting here in an airport. Casablanca. With me. Or are *you* a mirage?"

"No." He smiled faintly.

"I don't see any handcuffs."

"I'm on the honor system." Evan paused to consider the irony in that, but decided it was too grim for comment and continued quickly. "They're sending me home to the States."

"They?"

"The embassy. Fitzgerald."

"Oh yes," she said. "That nice Mr. Fitzgerald from Rabat." She said as though repeating a memorized phrase. A rough edge crept into her voice as she offered a brittle "I think you're putting me on!" But it hid a cry of despair—the final one before her acceptance of reality, of his reality and his whole situation.

"I wish I were, lady," Evan told her. "I really wish I were."

15

"AIR FRANCE FLIGHT 2006 to Paris is now boarding at Gate Two—Air France Flight 2006—"

Barbara began to pull herself together—or rather, to pull her things together, her armfuls of *tchachkes*. She saw that Deirdre and Evan were still engaged in their deadly serious dialogue and decided to leave them alone. She sensed that there was no way for her to help, perhaps even to understand. She got up and slowly started toward the tunnel that led to the boarding gate.

With infinite weariness and regret, Evan got up from the bench. Reluctantly, Deirdre stood up too and began to collect her things. The expression on her face so mirrored his that their unusual resemblance became, for the moment, truly remarkable.

In a sad, strained voice she asked him, "What happens in the States?"

He looked at her, "I'll be court-martialed."

Very taut. "And?"

"I go to prison."

Although she had known what was coming, Deirdre winced, as at a blow.

Her reaction threw him off-balance. He apologized gently. "I should've told you. In the beginning."

She bristled, unable to be comforted. "*Why?* You don't owe me any explanations."

"Deirdre—"

"Deirdre *what?*" Furiously she took a deep breath, and the strategy was successful—for no tears came. "You're right," she said. "I'm a girl you met on a train."

In flight from her warring emotions, she hurried across the waiting area.

Evan hurried after her. "Deirdre—"

Her long blonde hair waving above the green cape, Deirdre was conspicuously beautiful as she pressed into the anonymous crowd of passengers that moved slowly, chattering, through the tunnel toward the boarding gate. More people were clustered at the gate where a smartly uniformed clerk was examining their passes.

Evan caught up with Deirdre. Silently they walked on together and took their places at the end of the line of passengers who were waiting to board.

Very quietly Deirdre asked, "How long have you been gone? From the States?"

He frowned and looked around at the surrounding people, playing for time.

She pushed it. "I really want to know."

"Three years," he told her. "Three years and a few weeks."

The line moved slowly toward the gate, as, oblivious, Deirdre and Evan continued their dialogue.

"How did you end up in Marrakesh?" And, with an ironic small laugh, "I know, don't tell me it's a long story."

"I deserted from Japan," he said. "I was on something called Rest and Recreation. Then I got in touch with one of the peace groups in Tokyo, and they took care of me for a while."

In Arabic, ahead of them, the clerk was saying, "Have your boarding passes ready—" And, in French and then in English. "Please show your boarding passes—"

Reaching into her bag, fumbling about as though not quite sure what a boarding pass was, Deirdre finally came out with it, as Evan reached into his pocket for his.

Just in front of Evan stood a young Arab woman, a baby in her arms, her face a dark mask of confusion and some deeper fear or despair. Impossible to read her enormous eyes, Evan felt. Balancing the baby on one hip—she was very thin; he thought, her bones must have been sharp—she held the baby with one hand and with the other tried to open her purse.

Gesturing, Evan spoke to her. "Here, I'll hold him."

She stared: a blond American, a blond god traveling with his goddess, who spoke her language and offered help?

Firmly Evan took the child from her, as she mumbled a guilty thank-you.

But the baby was unimpressed with foreign gods and began to scream.

The woman moved to take him back; she murmured that he was too much trouble, all babies are sometimes too much trouble.

Evan reassured her. "No, it's all right."

Deirdre stared at the woman and at the baby with an uncharacteristic lack of sympathy or interest. Their world, their life were too remote from hers, and at the moment her own world was too much with her, much too much. She frowned at the still crying baby, unmoved by his huge dark teared eyes, and she asked Evan, "Then what happened?"

He gestured toward the baby—at which she frowned darkly. "I can hear you perfectly well."

Quietly he said, "I let the peace people send me to Moscow, which I don't think is going to do much for me in the States."

The Arab woman, smiling now, produced her boarding pass. With murmurs of thanks to Evan and croons of comfort to her child she took him back. The baby instantly stopped crying.

"What do you mean?" asked Deirdre.

His voice tightened. "Well, the Russians wined me and dined me, and I gave a few press interviews. And then, when I wore out my publicity value, the Russians said good-bye, and I went to Sweden."

For Deirdre the story had taken on the quality of a nightmare. Numbly she asked, "Sweden?"

He explained softly. "There was a whole colony of deserters there. The Swedish government gave us something called humanitarian asylum. They even gave us money to live on."

Having almost forgotten their destination, they were startled to realize they had reached the gate. The clerk stood waiting for Deirdre to show her pass.

She turned to Evan, "What does he want?"

"Your boarding pass."

Blinking in the sunlight, like confused people emerging from a cave, Evan and Deirdre began to cross the field to the waiting plane. They had slowed their pace, and Evan spoke very rapidly as though it was important to say as much as possible before getting aboard.

"It's cold in Sweden," he said. "The daylight ends at three in the afternoon." He shivered in the African sunlight, remembering that northern cold. "And whenever the political climate shifted two inches to the right it looked like that was going to be the end of humanitarian asylum. I got tired of being cold, and I got tired of being nervous. And anyway, I was never very good at being part of a group."

"And so—Marrakesh?"

They were approaching the plane, walking even more slowly, and the pace of their discourse had also slackened, as though they were running down.

Evan nodded. "Marrakesh. It seemed like a fairly safe place to get lost. And it was."

She smiled. "And warm."

"Right. Nice and warm."

"How did you live there?"

"Odd jobs. Listen lady, I've washed dishes in some very exotic places."

Her answering smile was faint. In silence they reached the ramp of stairs leading up to the plane. People were crowded around it in a loosely formed line that was moving very slowly. Evan and Deirdre took their places at the end.

Very intensely she asked, "Why did you *do* it?"

"Desert?"

She shook her head. "No, stupid. I mean why are you turning yourself in?"

"It's pointless not to."

She opened her mouth to speak, but then thought better of it. Then said, "Won't you get an amnesty?"

"Deirdre, amnesties are not for deserters, certainly not for a deserter who went to Moscow— you know, it's against the tradition: it's very un-American to desert—"

Deirdre grimaced.

"I'm tired of running," he said. "I want my life back, Deirdre."

She looked at him as though wanting to give him his life.

He went on. "Look, I used to think my deserting was a statement. You know? I really thought my staying away was saying something. About the war. About how wrong we were, and still are."

"But weren't you? saying something?"

"Well, it wasn't much of a statement, because nobody heard. The statements have all been made—it's too late."

They fell silent, helplessly silent, as the line of passengers inched its way up the stairs and crowded into the plane.

But just as they reached the door, Deirdre whispered to Evan, "The sound of one hand clapping?"

"You might say that." He smiled down at her.

16

PICKING THEIR WAY through bags and other people's legs, Deirdre and Evan made their way down the aisle of the first-class cabin. They found two seats near the rear of the plane, Evan stowed their hand luggage in the rack above, and they sat down.

From her window seat Deirdre could see nothing but the routine activity of the airfield: the flurry of mechanics, the dangerous speed of luggage trucks. She looked in the direction of where the sea must be and saw a blue haze that could have been simply air. Closing her eyes, she began —already—to remember Marrakesh. She saw again the sunset of the night before—God, was it possible?—a sunset that she saw before she had ever met Evan Bonner. She saw the terra-cotta city enflamed by the slowly dying rays. The tower with its high minaret. The city wall.

"Hey—"

She opened her eyes and turned around to Evan, who was fastening his seat belt. "Fasten yours," he told her.

Frowning, she clasped the belt and then leaned back in her seat. When she spoke it was from some private distance. "I went on a peace march once," she said. "It was February, and we marched up Fifth Avenue. There were thousands of people, really thousands. The marchers. The crowds watching." She looked over at him. "The people who organized the whole thing asked me to walk in front, with all the well-known faces. They wanted media coverage."

She had been speaking with an air that implied important further revelations. Evan waited for her to go on.

"It was very cold," she said. "*Very* cold. A lot of us ended up in a bar on Thirty-fourth Street. I got laid that night by a very famous liberal politician."

Very challenging, she waited for his response.

"Congratulations," and he laughed.

At that moment the jet motors started up, making further conversation impossible.

Like many large cities, Casablanca was seen at its best from high in the air: the tall buildings looked white, and the sea very blue. The dirt and the dirty shacks all disappeared.

Near the front of the plane, Barbara, for possibly the tenth time, squirmed about in her seat, her eyes searching the cabin. But even now, with everyone seated and strapped in, it was difficult to spot a particular face. Newspapers and hats as well as heads and hairdos interfered with her view. Barbara told herself that Deirdre was not so silly as to miss a plane and that if she *had* missed it, there was nothing at this point that she could do. She turned around again and thought she caught a glimpse of hair the color of Deirdre's hair, but she couldn't be sure.

"Champagne, madame?"

"What?" Barbara's attention swerved over to the aisle.

A trim stewardess stood there with a serving cart. "A glass of champagne, madame?"

Barbara shrugged and smiled. "Well, why not?" She accepted the glass that the girl filled for her, and she drank, having first made a toasting gesture to the air ahead of her.

Deirdre folded and refolded the cocktail napkin in her lap. Then she gave it up, dropped it, and turned to Evan. "But it's different now, isn't it?"

"What's different?"

The heavy hum of the engines shielded their voices from the rest of the plane, providing a cocoon of privacy.

"The war," Deirdre said. "We're almost out of it. Doesn't that change anything?"

"I'm still on the books. I always will be."

She picked up the napkin again. Fold. Refold. Then she held her hands absolutely still and tight as she asked, "Do you know how long a sentence you'll get?"

He nodded. "I'm fairly sure."

"Well? How long?"

"Five years."

She crumpled the napkin convulsively and closed her eyes.

"Hey, maybe three and a half, with good behavior."

She looked at him again.

"And I'm going to be very good," he said.

Below them now only the blue Atlantic glittered beneath the pale and couldless sky—a seemingly empty, endless sky.

"Five years for three?" Deirdre spoke angrily. "Even their goddam arithmetic stinks."

"I broke the law."

"*You* broke the law?"

He wiped at his forehead with a tired young hand. "Forget it," he said. "I've been through that argument a thousand times."

"But it's true! The *war's* illegal. You took a stand—on a stupid, corrupt, immoral war."

"Hey," he said. "You've got me pegged as a sort of hero. And I'm not."

"God, you're so—so *calm* about this."

"Deirdre—" His voice was taut, was anything but calm. "Deirdre, you spend a couple of years in exile, you just try it. You really learn to see the other guy's point of view." He looked at her, hard. "Come on, you think I just flipped a coin and decided to go back? I stewed around for months before I wrote the embassy."

"But then?"

He put both hands on the seat ahead of him,

gripping it hard. "Okay," he said. "You know how I finally managed it? I stopped feeling, that's how. No anger, no sense of right and wrong. No nothing. It's marvelous."

"Okay, so I was wrong." Deirdre sighed. "You're about as calm as a turkey in November."

He turned to her. "Look, couldn't we drop it?"

"Sure. I'm sorry I brought it up." She stared out the window at nothing.

Evan said, "Do you know *why* I don't want to talk about it?"

She turned toward him again.

"I'm scared, that's why. I'm scared that before I get to New York I'll change my mind again. And all that would do for me is take a few *more* years off my life."

"Champagne?" The stewardess with her cart had reached their seats, had turned her politely inquiring smile in their direction. "Monsieur, madame, champagne?"

Deirdre looked at her blankly, but Evan said "Sure, why not?"

The stewardess poured two glasses and handed them to Evan. He thanked her and gave a glass to Deirdre, as the stewardess moved her cart down to the next seat.

Deirdre eyed the liquid in her glass as though it were poison.

Evan caught the grimace and its intensity struck him as funny. "Cheer up," he said. "You can send me a box of cookies."

"You can go to hell," she told him and downed half her glass of champagne.

"But no grass in the brownies. I'm going to be very good."

17

ON THAT BUSY midafternoon, Orly Field had reached a peak of frenzy that could be equaled only at another international airport: the tight lines of people waiting to board the planes, the straggling lines of recent arrivals crossing the field, eyes strained toward the waiting area. The planes, except perhaps to the highly initiated, seemed interchangeable. The just-arrived plane from Casablanca could have been any plane at all.

Most of the passengers, including Barbara, had disembarked, and were boarding two airfield trams to take them to the terminal.

Barbara looked back at the plane, from which one or two passengers were still straggling out. Over and over, as she searched the faces, she reminded herself that if Deirdre was not on board there was absolutely nothing she could do. Frowning unhappily, she got on the second tram.

Inside the plane, where the very last passengers were collecting their luggage and leaving, Deirdre and Evan remained in their seats, as though their still-fastened seat belts locked them there. They did not look at each other, but neither did they move to get up.

Out of their silence Evan asked, "Can I see you tonight?"

"I don't think so."

His expression was undecipherable.

She added, "I mean, wouldn't you say that was asking for trouble?" Her glance was a challenge.

Judiciously he replied, "Not if we use our heads."

She tossed her head. "Forget it, Mr. Bonner. I think I've done my bit for the movement."

"You're a very tough lady, aren't you?"

She stared at him, and then cried out, "Could we please get out of here?" Furiously she unfastened the belt.

He waited for a moment, then he too unfastened his belt and got up to collect their hand luggage from above. Together—but not together —they walked toward the door, where the stewardess's smile had begun to freeze.

Evan spoke to her. "Miss?"

The smile unfroze. "Oui, monsieur?"

"They told me the airline would put me up for the night."

"Oui. There are two hotels. One here at the airport and one in Paris."

Evan glanced over at Deirdre, but she stepped out of the plane and headed down the stairs.

"What time does your plane leave tomorrow, monsieur?"

"Eight o'clock in the morning."

"It is sometimes difficult to get a taxi."

He looked at her. "Thank you, mademoiselle."

Surprisingly, after her angry exit, Deirdre was waiting for him at the foot of the stairs. He grinned at her, then shivered. "It's cold here."

"April in Paris. Haven't you heard? You *are* going in to Paris, aren't you?"

"I don't know yet."

They were walking toward a waiting tram, but now she stopped to face him squarely. "Have you ever *seen* Paris?"

"No."

She started walking again, and her voice was tremulous as she said, "It's the most beautiful city in the world, and it may not be here in five years."

They got onto the crowded tram, where they were greeted with general looks of impatience. Deirdre found a seat between two Arabs who did not look impatient, and Evan grabbed the strap that hung above her. Finally the stewardess came down the stairs of the plane and boarded the tram. The doors closed, and they started for the terminal building.

Jolting along, Deirdre and Evan rode in silence for a while; he watched her face, which for the moment was impossible to read. Then suddenly she looked at him and began speaking with an animation that was almost hysterical. "Do you know what you have to do tonight?" she said. "You have to go to St. Hilaire." She looked away from him, she narrowed her eyes, as her voice rose and just managed not to tremble. "It's this absolutely nutsy club in Montparnasse. Always a lot of sensational-looking girls there. You can pick one up and have a *marvelous* time."

"I may do just that." His voice was frozen.

An angry look. "Come on, say it like you're going to enjoy it."

Furious, he muttered, "Will you please knock it off?"

In that hostile silence they stared at each other until the tram drew up to the terminal building.

As they stepped off the tram, Evan asked Deirdre, "Are we on the same plane tomorrow?"

"No, I've just decided: I'm going to sleep in." Then she tossed at him, "If you do pick someone up, just make sure she's a brunette."

Evan and Deirdre emerged from the terminal to find Barbara heading the line of people who were waiting for cabs.

She called out to them, "Care to share a taxi with a fellow American?" Her voice held only a fraction of the anxiety and relief she felt on seeing them.

And once more the three of them were piled into a taxi together and headed toward a foreign city. Barbara bubbled, "Well, here we are again."

Deirdre ignored Barbara's cheerful chatter. "Yes, France again." She looked out the window: gloomy weather. "It always looks so—so French, doesn't it."

The Place de la Concorde was incredibly snarled with late afternoon traffic, somehow made worse by the sullen threat of rain. Their driver swore to himself and pushed his beret to one side: "The Crillon, you said, monsieur?"

Evan questioned Barbara.

"Yes, the Crillon."

Past the fountains with their small statues, the obelisk, then the cab began to slow down. "This is it?" Evan asked Deirdre.

She nodded, not looking at him.

They rode for a few minutes in silence and then stopped before the austerely elegant facade of the Crillon. The Corinthian colonnades, with graceful sculptures at the pediments, inspired at least an appreciative glance from most visitors but were lost on the present self-absorbed trio.

Deirdre jumped out of the cab, opening her door before the driver could get to her, and she started toward the arcade in front.

She was intercepted by the richly costumed doorman. "Miss McCluskey, Mrs. Newman. Welcome back."

"Thank you, Paul." She had miraculously remembered his name. She hurried into the arcade and stood, holding herself apart from Barbara and Evan.

The doorman and a bellman began to remove the luggage from the cab, as Barbara paid the driver.

Standing on the sidewalk with his knapsack, Evan spoke to Barbara. "Well, I guess this is where we say so long," he said.

"Oh? Won't we see you?"

"No."

"I feel like—like we've always been together," Barbara said.

He smiled at her. "So do I."

"Well, I want to thank you. I mean, for the shoe and everything." She smiled helplessly. "And good luck."

"Good-bye."

After a moment of hesitation Evan started over to where Deirdre stood. But at his approach she came back out to the curb, as if to supervise the luggage. Her face was tight; she avoided his eyes.

He took his knapsack from the luggage and shrugged. "Well, take care of yourself."

She still wouldn't look at him as she said, "I'll do that."

He could not quite leave. At last he said, "You know what I wish?"

She finally looked at him, but it was a frightened look. "I don't think you better tell me."

"If I did have a wish I'd—" He broke off abruptly, and muttered, "What's the use?"

For a moment longer he studied her, then he picked up his knapsack and walked resolutely away from her, as though he knew where he was going.

Deirdre stood watching him. A man walking out into the April Paris dusk. A man she met on a train.

"Nice boy." Barbara, at her side, spoke quietly.

The bellmen went on into the hotel, bearing their luggage, and Deirdre and Barbara followed.

Lightly, a conversational tone disguising her curiosity, Barbara asked, "Did you ever find out who he is? That business about the passports, I mean."

Deirdre thought for a few seconds. "No, I didn't," she said.

18

EVAN WALKED slowly along the Champs Elysées.
He passed the American Embassy without seeing
it, nor did he notice the Arc de Triomphe in the
distance ahead of him. He almost bumped into a
baby carriage that held a very small blond child.
The carriage was being pushed by a young couple
—obviously poor, obviously in love.

"Oh, pardon."

"*Rien, monsieur.*"

Smiling a little to himself, Evan turned to
watch them as they headed toward the Place, the
girl's arm lightly across her husband's back as he
pushed their child, his face turning to hers. The
lights and fountains of the Place. The facade of
the Crillon, with lighted windows in some of the
upper rooms. Evan unconsciously checked the windows, he was not sure for what; then abruptly he
turned and walked purposefully on.

From the window of her unlighted bedroom
Deirdre stared down at the Place: the lights, the
fountains, the lonely obelisk, the undiminishing

traffic. She looked at the sky, which seemed to show signs of clearing, but the sight of a single star, between clouds, did little to lighten her mood.

Then it was no longer dusk, but dark, and Deirdre was still at her window. At the sudden sound of the phone in the sitting room of their suite she started violently, but made no move to answer it.

"Hello?" Barbara, conscientious as ever, picked up the phone.

"Mario!" Barbara we delighted to hear from him.

Deirdre's body sagged when she heard Mario's name.

"You darling, but how did you know we were *here*?" Barbara's eager, affectionate voice responded to the charm of the caller.

Deirdre walked over to her bed and lay across it, inert, in the dim, still room.

"Yes, just for the night," Barbara ran on. "Morocco? Heaven. But the train broke down this morning. Can you believe it?"

Two people in a desiccated walled-in garden. "I just want you to touch me. It's a very simple request." "I'd go out of my skin."

Deirdre covered her eyes with her hand, shutting out the dark.

His knapsack checked in at the Invalides terminal, Evan strolled among the evening crowds on

the Place de l'Opéra. It was the stroll of a man
with no place to go; indecision rather than enjoy-
ment of the evening directed his pace. One night
in Paris. He examined the possibilities as though
Paris were a present he had not wanted.

In a quick-service restaurant he ordered a ham-
burger and enjoyed a wry private smile at the
irony of his choice.

Coming out, having left most of the food on his
plate, he resumed his aimless, joyless walk. Then
stopped abruptly, arrested by a face: Deirdre's,
her elusive half-smile enlarged on the glossy cover
of a magazine that hung at a bizarre angle, from a
kiosk on the corner.

"That sounds lovely," Barbara said into the
phone. "Let me ask Deirdre."

She put down the phone and went over to the
door of the bedroom. "Deirdre—Deirdre, sitting
in the dark?" She tried to keep the concern out of
her voice.

A mumbled yes came through to her.

"Deirdre, there's a gallery opening. Mario
wants us to go. Could be sort of fun, don't you
think?"

A moment. Then, "You go."

Barbara stood frowning to herself. With a tiny
shrug she went back to the phone. "Mario darling,
I'll talk to you a little later, okay?"

Then, knowing better but unable to stop herself, she recrossed the sitting room and stood at
the door of Deirdre's bedroom.

"Sweetie, what're you in the dark for?"

Deirdre sat up and rubbed at her eyes.

"Is anything wrong?"

"No," Deirdre lied. "I was just resting."

"I told Mario I'd call him back."

"Go ahead." Deirdre was vehement. "Really."

Barbara said, "It might be fun. It's a new sculptor. Nigerian. There'll be a lot of people you know."

"Yes, I'm *sure* there will be."

"I would like to go out," Barbara admitted. "When I get back to New York tomorrow, Charlie's mother's coming for a visit. That means three weeks quarantine."

"Don't you take her anywhere?" Deirdre was always curious about the inner workings of Barbara's marriage.

"Radio City. You know, all those girls—kicking, kicking, kicking."

At the Place du Théâtre, Evan stopped for a moment to get his bearings. It was almost curtain time, and all about him the chattering theater crowd hurried past in their fashionable clothes, with their bright eager faces.

Searching his mind for anything, any place that he had ever heard of in Paris, his eyes stopped at a sign that said Hotel Louvre. Of course—the museum. Would it be open at night, and if so, where was it? He began to sift through the passersby for a likely source of information.

He stopped an elderly gentleman who was walking more slowly than the rest, presumably not in a hurry to make a curtain.

"Sir, could you please tell me where the Louvre Museum is?" He spoke very slowly, overpronouncing his words in the hope of being understood.

The man looked at him blankly, with some irritation. "Eh?"

Evan repeated the question, more slowly yet and louder. "The Louvre Museum?"

"Young man," he was severely told, "my English is quite adequate. It is just that you speak in such an odd way. The Louvre is perhaps ten minutes from here. You go to the end of this block and then turn right, always right."

"Thank you very much."

The Louvre was indeed open. The recently cleaned exterior was flooded with light. Awed, Evan approached the magnificent palace and, avoiding a guided tour assembled there, he climbed the stairs and went in. Up more stairs, past the Venus, at which he hardly glanced.

As though looking for something—or someone —he hurried from room to room, rooms full of paintings so familiar they seemed reproductions. In one room he found himself trapped between two guided tours: one of Americans commenting in familiar accents of the Midwest; the other looked Swiss: diligent and dowdy, listening to their German guide. Wanting to avoid both of them, Evan was forced to look at the pictures.

Huge pink nudes, in fantastic attitudes of love. Golden clouds hung about in the background.

Flowers, rosy cupids with bows and arrows. More flesh.

Love?

And what was he doing there?

Ducking the Swiss he hurried from the room, out of the building and into the night.

19

THE GALLERY WAS narrow and austerely white, furnished with nothing but stands for the sculpture; it was almost a parody of a chic gallery. At the moment, a crowd of extremely well-dressed people milled about in that stylish space—for the most part older people in desperately good shape. Tans abounded: spring skiing, winter vacations in the tropics. There were extremely well-coiffed heads of hair, on men as well as women, and jewelry that was large and very simple and possibly priceless. The international rich.

The well-massaged, trim middle-aged women, one dark and French, the other a not-quite-faded English blonde, stood beside an exceptionally undistinguished sculpture: a moving construction of wood and metal. They were talking to the sculptor, a small and perfectly proportioned Nigerian, whose mod clothes, flamboyant tie, and wide flared pants were quite as fashionable as the ladies floor-length skirts—one wore pleated silk, the other plaid.

The sculptor spoke. "You see, I think for an

artist like myself this is the spirit of our times. Functionalism—" He floundered for an instant, but then, propitiously, was distracted by a greeting from a new arrival across the room. "Ah, excuse me," and he left the two ladies confronted with his sculpture and with each other.

"Did you notice those shoulders?" asked the British blonde.

"But of course." The French lady smiled discreetly.

In another corner, beside an equally meretricious piece of sculpture, Barbara spoke earnestly to Mario. "But I think it's interesting that he *isn't* ethnic."

"It would be more interesting if he had talent." Mario was an older Italian, a man of great substance with an opulent tie and weary, circled eyes.

"Mario," chided Barbara.

A waiter appeared from nowhere and filled their empty glasses again with champagne.

Deirdre, in still another corner, was talking with Gilles, an extraordinarily handsome Frenchman. In his forties, Gilles was dark and trim indeed—he looked like a movie star or a jet-set celebrity, at the very least; one tried to place his face. He wore dark glasses, always, but it generally took people quite a while to realize that he was totally blind.

"I'm glad you're here," Deirdre told him— Deirdre slinky in her long pale green and beige jersey gown, the colors seeming to flow into each other—Deirdre slinky and very pretty and unquestionably sad.

"Are you?" he asked. "You promised to phone me when you came back to Paris."

"I'm sorry, Gilles. We got in so late."

"Is Ron here? I don't see him." Gilles often said "see" in this way, by which he meant his own special sort of awareness; he did not sense the presence of Ron in that room.

"Didn't I mention it? Ron went off to the Sahara."

Gilles smiled. "The explorer."

"Yes. He'll spend an hour and a half taking pictures of the nomads. Very rough-grained and elemental—that sort of thing. Then he'll tell all his friends that that's the kind of work he really wants to do."

"You are not very charitable."

She sniffed. "Ron doesn't need my charity."

Gilles moved his hand along the edge of a sculpture stand until he found his glass: his single gesture of blindness, which was somehow shocking. He sipped at his champagne.

"Gilles, why do you come to these nitwit things?" Deirdre frowned at the room at large as she spoke.

"I know there will be people. Life." He turned toward her, as though he could see her troubled face. "You are not very happy with the world tonight."

She sighed. "It's true, isn't it? The blind do have a sixth sense."

He smiled slightly. "Not at all. Only more anxiety." Then, "*Are* you happy?"

The two middle-aged ladies, the English and the French, approached Deirdre and Gilles, speaking intently to each other, with the quick nods and hushed tones usually reserved for decisions on the fate of the world.

The Frenchwoman said, "I am told she is a lesbian. From a place called Wyoming."

"Wyoming? I don't believe I've heard of it."

"You know the cowboys and Indians. Buffalo." Conspiratorially she lowered her voice. "You will meet her at lunch next week."

As the women moved majestically past Deirdre and Gilles, Deirdre asked, "Life? People?"

Barbara and Mario came over to join them. Mario seemed to be continuing an argument. "It's not enough simply to be American," he said. "Everything has changed. Now the dollar must compete."

Barbara spoke anxiously. "But that's healthy, isn't it? Economically, I mean."

"Yes, it is healthy. But is it comfortable?"

Barbara turned to Deirdre, "Help me, Deirdre, Mario's analyzing our country again."

"*Are* we going to dinner soon?" Deirdre enquired.

Mario was instantly chivalrous. "Where would you like to go, my sweet?"

But Deirdre didn't answer him either. Her attention had been caught by a scene a few feet to their right: the sculptor was greeting five Vietnamese gentlemen of varying ages. They were impeccable, in dark suits with conservative ties, and they seemed to know quite a few people in the room. They were totally at home in the rich milieu. As Deirdre watched them, a waiter approached with champagne, and they all helped themselves from his tray.

"Who *are* those men?" Deirdre's question was directed to no one in particular.

Barbara and Mario turned to look, and Gilles turned too.

"The Vietnamese," said Deirdre.

Mario frowned. "I have seen them before. I think they are from the peace talks."

"Are they North or South?"

Mario turned to look again, and frowned again. "It is no longer easy to know. They have all been in Paris so long."

With a lot of bowing and handshaking all around, the sculptor parted from the Vietnamese. They, in their turn, detained the waiter, who refilled all their glasses with champagne.

"I understand that now both sides go to the same tailor," continued Mario.

"They don't look very ravaged, do they?" By now Deirdre's voice had risen. "I mean, you can hardly tell where the napalm hit."

Mario shrugged, but he watched her cautiously as he spoke: "Every country must have its diplomats."

"Then why aren't they diplomating? They've all held the world on its ear for seven years. Why are they wasting time looking at a lot of crappy sculpture?"

They watched as the Vietnamese continued to sip their wine, looking about the gallery and occasionally nodding to friends.

Still speaking rather loudly, Deirdre said, "Well, I suppose if I could stay this close to the Dom Perignon I wouldn't be in such a hurry either to tear-ass home."

Gilles' gentle voice pleaded, "Deirdre, what is it? I do not know what troubles you so tonight."

She turned to him. "It's too bad you can't see them, Gilles. You may know them. I doubt if they've always been in such exalted jobs."

By this time both Mario and Barbara were staring at her, with puzzled, uncomfortable expressions, but Deirdre went right on. "One or two of them are old enough to have been at Dienbienphu," she said.

Horrified, Barbara mouthed a silent "Don't."

But Gilles spoke evenly. "And if they were?"

Deirdre's voice was near the breaking point. "I was just thinking: wouldn't it add up just about perfectly if one of those well-dressed gentlemen had fired the thing that blinded you?"

Barbara, shocked, blurted out. "Deirdre, stop it!"

Deirdre seemed not to hear. "Well, doesn't that even bother you?"

Still even and gentle, Gilles spoke after a small hesitation. "I will tell you something about blindness, Deirdre. There comes a time when you forget how you came to be blind. You only know that you are."

In an appalled silence, Deirdre absorbed his comments. The others shifted restlessly.

It was Mario who finally spoke, with a heartiness that did not ring quite true. "Deirdre, I have friends here in Paris," he said. "Textile men from Stuttgart. They are anxious to meet you."

Deirdre didn't respond. She was still watching the Vietnamese, who were united at that moment in admiring one of the sculptures.

Mario went on trying in his friendly, attractive manner. "They are planning an international campaign. Magazines. Television."

"Money money money, luv," said Barbara, who was regarding Deirdre anxiously.

Deirdre looked at Barbara and at Mario as if she were not quite sure who they were.

Mario began to sound uncertain. "We will meet them after dinner. You will have to give me an agent's commission," he tried to tease.

Deirdre stared at them and then looked wildly all about the room, still without acknowledging that she had heard anything they had said to her.

20

ANCHORED NEAR Pont Neuf, the Bateau Mouche, the broad, low-lying pleasure boat, was so brilliantly illuminated that one wondered how nocturnal sightseers on board could see out into the darkness of the city. Nevertheless, it attracted a considerable crowd; people were boarding, and others stood in line at the ticket window.

Near the window, but apart from the crowd, Evan stood and read from an English-language brochure, *Paris By Night*: The names of bridges and a capsule of their history. The illuminated fountains at the Trocadero. The Eiffel Tower. He stopped reading and studied the crowd. Couples. Old people, young people, heavy middle-aged people, but all couples. With a decisive gesture he tossed the brochure into a trash can.

Then he scanned the dock for something that was not there; he hurried on as though he had at last made up his mind about something. Even if it was only to find a phone booth. A few blocks away he located one, well furnished with directories.

Which Evan eagerly opened, scanning the pages for an address.

The Club St. Hilaire. The overwhelming thing was the noise: blaring decibels of rock music seemed to push out against the walls, and thousands of impossible conversations wound above and below the music—conversations between hundreds of people, mainly very young, jammed into the available space, moving and laughing and obviously having a good time. What one could glimpse of the decor was futuristic: geodesic shapes, tubular steel staircases that led from one level to another, a lot of clear plastic. A disk girl, in a glass elevator-booth.

Very much a stranger in a strange land, Evan made his way through the club, an untouched drink in his hand. He was vividly aware of his years of exile, during which, he supposed, all this had been going on, accumulating momentum and noise.

Couples danced violently at each other, their gestures and gyrations wild. At a large table, full of people, everyone laughed as though at a single joke, but how could they have heard a single joke? A big red-haired girl danced alone, her eyes half-closed, her body a total response to the music. A fat hippie boy came by with a tiny monkey on a ribbon, which he introduced to a group at a table.

Awkwardly Evan looked about for a place to sit down, but the empty spaces were all next to some lively group. He headed toward what he thought was an isolated corner, in the dark, but as he approached he saw two lovers there, their hands all over each other. He turned abruptly to the other direction.

And saw, on the spiral staircase, the back of a head with a sheaf of dark blonde hair, the color of Deirdre's hair. His stomach clutched. Then she turned: a pretty young French girl. Not Deirdre, but also tall and lithe.

The girl smiled at him, and Evan returned her smile, feeling discomfort in the muscles of his face. He nodded to her and moved on, first pausing for a moment at the table where the monkey was. It pranced about, then stopped to nibble delicately at a young girl's hand. Shrieks of laughter. "Albert, he's too much! Wild!"

Evan lost interest.

He started up a crowded staircase to another level, moving aside as he ascended to let couples pass. People paid hardly any attention to him, and Evan began to have an odd sense that he was invisible as well as out of place.

On the upper level it was somewhat less crowded. With relative ease Evan wandered over to the booth where the disk girl—a voluptuous brunette—was very busy at her work. Still, with his curious sense of being invisible, he stared at her for several minutes. She finally looked up, and he smiled at her.

She smiled back, but with such a quick meager

smile that Evan wished she hadn't bothered. She pressed a button, still inside her booth, and descended out of sight, without a backward look.

Evan went over to another staircase and started down, again to be buffeted by passing couples who seemed hardly to see him.

At the bottom of the stairs stood the French girl, the not-Deirdre blonde, who did see Evan. And smiled again.

This time more comfortably Evan returned her smile, and she walked over to him. "Are you enjoying St. Hilaire?"

Surprised and mildly pleased, "You speak English," he said.

She nodded seriously. "You are American?"

She was wearing a very simple black dress—much too simple a dress for Deirdre to wear, Evan decided.

He asked, "How did you know?" and they both laughed at that.

She looked up at him. "Would you like to dance?"

"Uh-why don't we have a drink?"

"All right."

Efficiently she spotted a place to sit, across the dance floor, and touching Evan's arm lightly she pointed it out, and she began to lead him to it, dexterously threading through the crowd.

But after a moment Evan stopped, suddenly riveted to where he stood, as, utterly incredulous, he stared at an upper level.

Deirdre. Really Deirdre, watching him, her smile teasing and amused. Lovely Deirdre in a sumptuous black cape.

When Evan finally let himself believe that it was really she, a huge glowing grin spread all over his face.

Uncomprehending, the French girl pulled at his arm.

He turned to her. "Listen, will you—I—uh—" But it was too much to explain even if she did speak English and he gave it up. "Excuse me," and he started toward Deirdre.

Frowning, the girl watched him go. Then she shrugged; after all, he was not the only good-looking boy in the room. Still he was far more attractive than most, and she did have sort of a thing about Americans.

Urgency made Evan much more nimble than before, and he darted through the crowd as though he had spent the last few years running interference in just such places.

Deirdre began to move toward him along her balcony; she pressed herself against the railing and seemed to glide along it.

Both fighting through the crowd—they reached each other at last, laughing and out of breath.

Deirdre spoke first. "You bastard," she said. "She's not a brunette."

He was serious. He took her hands in his and said, "I'm glad you did it. Boy, am I glad you did it."

Lightly, and not quite convincingly, she said,

"It's only for tonight, you know. When tomorrow comes, you go one way, and it—"

Gently, "Shut up," he told her.

His arms reached out for her, and she came to him, and their mouths and the length of their bodies met and held in a prolonged embrace. And all about them the music blared on, people danced and laughed and talked as though nothing momentous had occurred.

21

STILL STANDING ON that improbable staircase, Evan gradually released Deirdre from his close embrace.

Looking up at him, she asked, "When does your plane leave?"

"Eight A.M. What time is it now?

They were both still out of breath, and they still regarded each other with some disbelief.

Ten, ten-thirty," Deirdre told him. "Where do you want to go?"

"You know something, lady? It just doesn't matter."

They reached out for each other, to hold and kiss each other again and again.

Then Evan said, "Come on, let's get out. Let's get a cab, and go—go somewhere."

Near the great square stone facade of Notre Dame, their taxi pulled up at the bridge, and Evan and Deirdre got out. Evan started to pay the driver but Deirdre stopped him.

"I'll get it," she commanded. "You look at the scenery."

"Hey—"

"Just do as I say."

Playfully he cuffed at her arm. "Say, you're pretty bossy."

But he did as she said. He went over to the balustrade to look at the church. After she had paid the driver, Deirdre joined him there, and after a moment Evan was studying her again.

"Will you please look?" she said. She was very urgent; she was not entirely kidding.

"I did look. It's great."

"No, I mean *really* look." She had his arm. "It's Notre Dame. One of the wonders of the world. By the time you're free it may be a parking structure—"

They looked at each other, shadows of pain across both their faces. Evan turned from Deirdre to Notre Dame, telling himself that it was beautiful—even, dutifully, trying to memorize it: the two towers, round stained-glass window, huge carved door. Then he turned back to Deirdre.

"Got it filed away," he said but his intense, searching look revealed that Deirdre was the subject of his memory bank.

His concentration on her discomfited Deirdre; to divert him she asked if he had eaten.

"Kind of. Did you?"

"More or less."

He asked her. "Are you hungry?"

"No, are you?"

"No."

Helplessly Deirdre said, "Evan, do you want to go back to my room?"

He reached and touched her face. "Not yet. Not for a little while."

She cried then, "There *is* no time—there's no time for anything. . . ."

Weeping, she turned her back to him and held the balustrade.

After a moment Evan went over to her; he turned her around to face him. "Now listen," he said, "there's eight hours. Some people never get eight hours—"

"I don't even know how to begin!" she wept.

He held her very close. "Relax. It's already begun."

He took her hand, and the two of them started to walk, hand in hand, slowly, beside the slow and gleaming river.

"What did you do?" Evan asked her.

"Tonight?"

"Uh huh."

"God, don't ask. . . . What did you do?" she asked him.

"Oh, I wandered around." He laughed—from his present perspective almost anything could seem funny. "I nearly went to a movie."

Deirdre winced. "Oh no." On a single impulse they stopped walking. They faced each other, and Deirdre buried her face in his chest. "I'm *sorry*," she said. "I really am. We could've missed each other completely."

He took her chin in his hand and lifted it; he

was smiling as he said, "You sure we ought to spend time worrying about the past?"

They walked on, through the frantic teeming, traffic-ridden St. Germain, past restaurants and clubs and gaudy fantastic shops, past a thousand people whom they did not see.

Reaching the Air Terminal, at Invalides, they crossed the almost deserted lobby and went over to the bank of lockers. Evan inserted the key and took out his knapsack, from which he extracted a sweater. He put it on, and smiling at Deirdre as his head emerged, kissed her as though they had been apart.

Recrossing the lobby, they passed a closed kiosk —again, with Deirdre's picture hanging from it at an angle.

Deirdre laughed. "Talk about fools' faces."

Evan asked her, "You like being a model?"

"I like the attention," she admitted, her chin defiantly out. "And I like being rich."

"*Are* you rich?"

She laughed. "This week I am."

Disingenuously he said, "You must meet a lot of interesting people."

Deirdre caught his tone, and she teased him. "Just what are you driving at, Mr. Bonner?"

He admitted, "Interesting men."

"Sure," she told him. "That's why I proposition strangers."

He drew her close beneath his arm as they continued out of the terminal.

Pont Alexander III. "I think this is my favorite bridge," said Deirdre. "Or Pont Neuf. But look, isn't it elegant?"

"You're elegant," he told her. "A very elegant lady."

"Evan, look at Paris!"

"Okay, okay!" He glanced back at Les Invalides, at the great dome and the wide space of grass leading up to it, the Grande Allée, and then ahead to the trees on the Right Bank, the anonymous shapes of famous buildings and all the lights. Then, having conscientiously inspected Paris, he resumed their earlier conversation. "But Ron?" he said. "Ron and Marcus?"

"The fact is," Deirdre told him, "I wanted a baby."

"Did you love him?"

"Ron?" Gazing down at reflected lights that danced on the surface of the water, Deirdre thought about it. "I don't think Ron and I ever loved each other. We were—were were *tchachkes* in each other's lives."

"Ouch—"

Affectionately she studied his face. "You've never done that, have you?" At that moment she felt considerably older than he. "You've never— just filled in space with somebody?"

He shrugged.

"Well, there was the so-called appropriateness of it all," Deirdre said. "The photographer-model thing—we looked good together."

He grinned. "I didn't think so at all."

She laughed at that, and the bitterness left her voice as she went on. "So, except for Marcus I guess that's the story of my life."

"I'm not sure I believe that, McCluskey."

They had begun slowly to walk across the bridge, but now Deirdre stopped and faced him as she said, "Listen, I'd better tell you something about me. I've always been positive that love is a fiction."

He looked at her evenly, which she found unaccountably unsettling.

"I've proved it, Evan," she told him. "More times than I want to remember."

Waiting for a reaction she looked up at him.

"Okay, you told me that legend once today." That was all he said.

She shook her head, and they moved on again, turning left at the other side of the bridge, to walk through the narrow park of plane trees, mysterious in the dark.

"Anyway," said Deirdre, "I didn't want to marry Ron, but I did want a baby. And he was there."

Admiringly, "You don't lack for nerve," he commented.

"I really thought I was different from the rest of the world. I was nineteen and healthy. I made a hundred thousand dollars that year. I figured I knew the answers to everything."

He asked her, "You regret it?"

"Oh no. I love Marcus, I really do. He's the best

thing in my life. But that doesn't do much for him. I'm not a very good mother."

"How so?"

"It's true. I'm not. I cheat in all the crummy little ways. When I'm away from him I feel guilty and when I'm with him too long I'm antsy to get away."

He asked her gently. "Don't a lot of mothers feel that way?"

Her voice rose. "A lot of mothers have husbands. A lot of mothers can share the guilt."

They had emerged from trees to a tree-lined well-lit sidewalk. The diminishing evening traffic streamed on the wide boulevard; above and ahead of them large buildings loomed dimly.

"I can throw baseballs to Marcus till hell freezes over," Deirdre said. "It's not the same thing." She reflected for a moment. "I think if you're going to break the rules in this world," she said, "you damn well better have a very cold heart."

She looked at him, remembered, and said very quietly, "Oh Christ, you know that better than I do."

22

OUTSIDE A SMALL restaurant, narrow, high-ceilinged, and discreetly lit, Deirdre and Evan stopped to scan the posted menu.

He said, "I guess we should eat?"

"I guess."

But the urgency for talk was more pressing: in eight hours, so much to say.

"I was planning to go to med school," Evan told her. "An uncle of mine's a doctor. Nice guy. He wanted me to practice with him."

"Are you still going to do it?"

"Who knows? I could be over thirty when I'm sprung."

The restaurant was classically Parisian: a lot of dark wood and very white linens on the tables, a single candle on each table. A plump smiling woman at the cash register, and several elderly waiters who did not hover. There were only two other couples in the place.

Impatiently looking over the long menu—hand-written, in purple script—Deirdre and Evan decided on a camembert and some fruit, an Alsatian white wine.

"1966—let's really do it," said Deirdre.

"Okay."

The waiter brought the tall green chilled bottle, and they toasted each other with a silent gesture.

And went on talking.

Somewhat abruptly Deirdre asked, "Do you have a girl somewhere?"

"Of course not—I would've told you."

"Would you?" She narrowed her eyes. "I'm not sure I would have."

"Why not?"

"I don't know. I'm still not sure we have to know everything about each other."

The fruit and cheese arrived, with bread and pale curls of butter.

"You know something?" Evan said. "You talk a good fight."

"Okay." She smiled and sipped her wine. "But there have been girls, haven't there."

"Sure."

"In Sweden?"

"Sweden. Morocco. Girls are nice to guys in my situation. Lots of sympathy—lots of free room and board. It's probably easier to be nice to someone when you know there isn't any future." Thinking: Irene, Renee, Ursula, and Nora who was almost as lovely as Deirdre—almost and therefore not.

She flared, "If you're talking about me—"

"Listen, if I were, I'd *tell* you I was."

"I guess you would, at that." She simmered down somewhat. "I stand corrected, sir." But she couldn't let it alone. "What happened with these girls?" she asked.

"Nothing special."

He offered her an apple. She shook her head, and he began to pare it as he spoke: "They wanted to get on with their lives, that's all. They married Swedes or Moroccans, or at least they started looking for a Swede or a Moroccan. A couple of them just went away to school. After a while —well, it wasn't their fault, but I really felt like a stud."

Deirdre winced, "I guess I asked for all this."

"Had enough?" He grinned at her.

"Enough," she told him, and she held out her glass for more wine. "This is so good—Evan, you have to remember this taste."

"Along with everything else?"

"Along with everything else." Then she asked, "Do your parents know you've turned yourself in?"

He nodded.

"How do they feel about it?"

"I suppose they're glad that it's over with." He looked away from her then; unhappily he looked all around the restaurant.

"Evan, what's wrong?"

"Nothing." But then, "Oh, my dad'll be okay," he said. "I mean, he's one of those people who really believe you have to take the consequences for what you do."

Deirdre spoke very quietly. "Knowing you, that's no big surprise."

"It's going to be harder for my mother." He went on with a certain humor in his voice. "She used to write me letters at first: couldn't I go back and say it was a mistake, that I was a conscientious objector or something? Then she tried to live with it. She joined peace groups, wrote congressmen. But that wasn't her thing either. She's really just a lady who loves her family and likes things orderly." He stopped for a moment, recalling his mother. "I know it doesn't make sense, but it really bugs me that she's going to have a son in prison." He paused. "Her letters make me sad," he said.

Very softly, Deirdre said, "It makes sense."

Walking again slowly, hand in hand, they came to a small square, a neighborhood *place* dominated by a monument: two soldiers, one British, one American, from World War II. Leisurely, mildly curious, they walked over to it and bent to see the inscription.

Deirdre pulled at Evan's hand impatiently. "Let's go on."

"But what does it say?"

"Do you really want to know?"

He nodded.

In a flat, deprecating tone she translated: "To the noble allies of France, the brave men who gave their lives for liberation. August, 1944." She looked at him. "Satisfied?"

Again, he nodded, and they continued on out of the square, on to a major boulevard, from which they could see the illuminated Arc de Triomphe.

Evan spoke from the private depths of his thoughts. "You know, it must've been easier in 1944. To give your life—or to take someone else's."

"I guess."

"Easier just to be in the army."

"I don't even understand how someone like you ever let yourself get drafted."

"That was four years ago," he told her. "I was a different guy."

The Arc had disappeared behind their backs; unconsciously they were heading toward the Place de la Concorde.

"I didn't ask questions," Evan said. "Where I came from nobody did. West Virginia, remember? I figured the army was something I had to do and that the kids who didn't want to go were dirty long-haired hippies."

"What changed your mind?"

"A lot of things. Just being in Vietnam was the beginning."

Gently she asked him, "What was it like, Evan?"

He gestured helplessness: impossible to tell what it was like. "It was as if—as if all of a sudden life had gone crazy. Half the guys were stoned out of their minds, and the other half talked about 'gooks' and 'body counts.' And you'd hear about things—the wrong village being leveled—the corruption—My Lai. But you know, for a while it still seemed as if I was *supposed* to be there."

"Till you killed someone?"

Startled, he looked at her. Then nodded.

"How did it happen?"

He shook his head.

She insisted. "No, tell me."

"It was nothing—special," he began. "He was just there one day in the jungle, right in front of me. I knew he'd get me if I didn't shoot. It seemed so *stupid* for us to be there like that, but I fired." He looked at her. "He wasn't a person any more. His body was just—useless."

Soothingly Deirdre touched his arm, but Evan went on, agitated, so that even his walk was faster, and she had trouble keeping up with him. "You know, sometimes I have this—this daydream that one day I'll find his family and try to explain. I know they won't forgive me but I guess I kid myself. I keep thinking we can be some kind of friends."

"Evan—"

He broke out angrily. "I'll never find those people, not now. And that's where I owe my dues. Not to some clown in Washington. I was right. God damn it, I was right, and now I'm going to say I was wrong."

"Evan—" Deirdre pulled at his arm. This time he stopped, and she put her arms around him. "Evan," she said again.

"Yes?"

"Let's go home."

He nodded, and they started to walk fast again.

Suddenly they broke into a run—at first a playful jog, and then they were caught up in it, running toward Concorde and her hotel, leaving the small square with the monument and the Arc de Triomphe far behind.

23

THE FOUNTAINS OF the Place de la Concorde were quiet as Deirdre and Evan crossed the street, and the street was quiet: emptied of traffic. Dark.

At the desk in the lobby of the Crillon the concierge was half-asleep at his desk, but by habit alert to the slightest sound. He bolted upright as Deirdre and Evan approached him; he straightened up and adjusted his tie. "Good evening, Miss McCluskey. There are some messages for you."

Deirdre took the key, and the message slips from him; she murmured *"Merci"* as she dropped the papers in the wastebasket, with a sly grin at Evan, then *"Bonne nuit."*

The concierge watched as they walked over to the elevator, silent on the heavy carpeting. He frowned: that shaggy young man, with elegant Mademoiselle McCluskey, going up to her room at such an hour? Then he stifled all judgment with a shrug. To their backs he said, *"Bonne nuit,"* and he returned to his dozing.

Deirdre and Evan hurried toward the elevator, where an American husband held the door open for his wife. The husband was clean-shaven, short-haired, and very thick about the waist. His eyes were small and close together, his tie very narrow. His wife had tightly knotted gray hair, a pursed mouth, and a shapelessly corseted body. Deirdre and Evan got into the car with them, the other Americans, and Deirdre pressed the button for her floor. The door closed, and the car rose in a silence that was heavily fraught with mutual awareness.

Deirdre couldn't stand it. Quite formally she turned to Evan, and said, "You know, before we get to the room I think we ought to settle on the price."

The American woman gulped noisily, then tightened her mouth into an even smaller line, while her husband cleared his throat. Evan looked murderously at Deirdre, who smiled back charmingly.

The elevator stopped, and with no parting exchange between the two couples, Deirdre and Evan got out. Almost doubled with silent laughter, Deirdre fled down the corridor.

Evan followed. "Fun-ny. Oh, you're a really funny lady, you are," and he rapped her sharply across the ass.

"Ouch!"

She darted ahead again, tossing him the room key as she did so. "Catch!"

He missed the key. Deirdre watched him stop and stoop to pick it up, and at that she darted into another corridor.

When he looked up she was gone. "Hey—

Deirdre?" Then, "Oh, for God's sake, Deirdre."
He strode over to the intersection of the corridors,
then stopped, trying to determine which direction. Loudly he whispered, "Come on, knock it
off."

No answer.

He chose at random and started down a corridor. More loudly he whispered, "Okay, so you're
the funniest girl in Steubenville."

Again no answer, and he turned and started
along another corridor when he saw her in a re-
cessed alcove, giggling, very amused with herself.

He started toward her. "Say, what was all that
about?"

But at his approach her whole mood changed,
like the sudden turning of a page. Her amusement was gone, and was replaced by something
she couldn't hide.

Evan asked, "What's wrong?" Coming up close,
staring at her, "You're frightened!" he exclaimed.

Her face indeed tight with fear, her eyes enormous and haunted, she nodded dumbly.

With great tenderness he took her in his arms,
and very gently he kissed her face and then her
mouth.

At last releasing each other, they walked toward
Deirdre's room, where Evan unlocked the door.
Inside, in the darkness, Deirdre pointed toward
Barbara's bedroom and then put that finger across
her lips. Evan pulled her to him, and they kissed
again.

In Deirdre's bedroom, with infinite slowness,

infinite tenderness, they undressed each other, standing in the dark; her long fingers unbuttoned his shirt, his hands lifted the top of her dress as her hand moved tenderly down his back, and still standing there beside her bed, they kissed.

Then Deirdre pulled a little away from him; holding a light coverlet up to her body, she opened the draperies and the shutters halfway and gestured for Evan to come over. Together at the window in the half-light they looked down at the quiet, deserted Place: the fountains stilled, lights dimmed, the empty street.

Evan pulled the draperies closed and undid the pins that held her hair. She dropped the coverlet, and, finally naked together, they went over to the bed and got in, and, very slowly, with a sort of ceremoniousness, they began to touch and kiss each other. To move together, to be together.

Two people.

24

ALONE IN HER BED, covered by a single sheet, Deirdre wept. Minutes passed, and still she cried, and then the bathroom door opened, and Evan came out.

As he moved through the dark toward the bed, he caught the vibrations. Asked, "Are you all right?"

"Sure."

He turned on the night lamp. She rubbed at her eyes and looked away. "Don't."

"Hey—" Troubled, he looked down at her.

She insisted. "I can't stand the glare."

He studied her for a moment, then turned off the lamp. He got into bed and held her close to him.

She moved back, and in the half-light he could still see a glitter of tears across her eyes. She asked, "You want to know how you rate on a scale of ten?"

"No, I don't."

"Was it those Arab girls? Did they teach you a lot? My God, they seemed so demure and—"

"Deirdre, stop it!"

Stopped by his anger, she looked at him.

"You were in the same place I was," he told her.

Seriously she nodded. Then her face softened, and the posture of her body. They moved together, kissed slowly, lingeringly—until, again, their bodies became less slow and tender, became frantically driven.

Faint dawn light filtered through the closed shutters, as Deirdre lay in Evan's arms. Idly she combed her fingers through his hair and asked, "What time is it?"

"Around four, I guess."

She yawned, curling a fist against her mouth.

"You're tired."

She murmured. "No."

"Go to sleep," he urged.

She protested, "But I don't want to *sleep*."

He touched her cheek, slowly caressed it.

Sleepily, "Don't do that," she told him. "Pinch me or something." Her eyes closed and he continued to caress her cheek.

"Please," she said, but she was really asleep.

As Deirdre slept with her head lying on his arm, Evan stared at the ceiling; he told himself that sleep would do him more good at this moment than serious thought, but he was unable to stop his mind. He also told himself that this was an impossible moment for major decisions, but still his thoughts remained serious.

At last pure physical restlessness set in, and he carefully disengaged his arm from Deirdre's sleeping head. Watching her face for any faint sign of waking, he got out of bed. He put on his pants and looked around the room, but nothing offered itself—there was nothing to do. He sat down in a chair that faced the bed, but at that moment to be confronted with Deirdre was to be confronted with his own most difficult thoughts. After a moment he got up and went over to the window and opened the draperies wide enough to look outside.

The Place was still quiet, the fountains immobilized. A small French car drove past, very slowly, as though not to disturb that silent hour. And then another, larger, soundless car. At the eastern edge of the gray night sky, above where Notre Dame must be, the faintest glimmering of dawn had begun, a yellow stain of light seeping into the gray.

Evan watched the gradual lightening of the sky and wrestled with the contents of his head.

When he turned around to check, Deirdre was still sleeping, and the room had begun to fill with an eerie half-light. He resumed his musing window watch.

But Deirdre soon awoke; she lay quietly watching him for quite a while, until he started to close the draperies. She sat up, using her elbow as a prop. "It's all right. I'm awake."

Arrested, he looked at her. "How *are* you?"

Her expression said everything and nothing at all.

She couldn't bear to speak.

Evan began to stammer. "I—I'm late," and he went to get his shirt.

"Evan?"

He moved toward her but stopped.

"What would happen if you didn't go back?" Her level, deadly serious look and voice.

Terrified of what must come next, he told her, "I don't know."

"If you want to stay, I'll stay with you."

Out of the variety of feelings that threatened to overwhelm him, he chose the easy one: "You're a nice lady, McCluskey."

"I mean it."

"I know." Despair lowered his voice.

He picked up his shirt and put it on.

"It's not impossible," Deirdre said.

Not looking at her, he muttered, "I don't think we'd even better think about it." In the ensuing silence he searched for his shoes and socks, which he had no memory of removing, much less placing anywhere. Improbably, they were under a chair. He concentrated on putting them on, as though it were an important task.

Deirdre's cry fractured the silence: "There are planes all day!"

He stared at her.

"You get a better cell if you get there early?"

Evan closed his eyes against this impossible and unavoidable confrontation.

More calmly, Deirdre went on. "I'm sorry, but

I'm not going to be stiff-upper-lipped about this."

Dumbly he nodded, and she waited for him to make some move.

When he did not, she spoke very softly. "Talk to me—*please*?"

"Not here—I can't."

She said, "Okay, I'll get dressed."

She got out of bed and went over to the dressing table. He came to stand beside her, and for a moment, side by side, they regarded each other in the wide ornamented mirror.

"It's uncanny," Deirdre said. "We sort of look alike."

Two faces shaped the same, blue eyes and fine blond hair. Two young faces shadowed with the same fatigue.

25

AS HURRIEDLY AS if they had a destination, Evan and Deirdre rushed through the lobby of the Crillon, past another concierge who raised his head and scowled at everything about them, including their total failure to see him. Deirdre wore a long plaid skirt, a high black sweater. Evan was slightly more rumpled than before.

Movement relieved some of Evan's tension, and he hurried Deirdre across the still deserted Place, toward the Tuileries. There, on the tidy graveled paths, they slowed their pace somewhat in keeping with the decorous spaces that surrounded them. The park was entirely empty of people, and leaves glistened in the chilled dawn air, still moist from the night just past.

Deirdre's voice was anxious and contained a note of pleading. "If you stayed, would they make things worse for you? Because you've turned yourself in?"

"I don't know." He didn't look at her.

"Would they send someone after you?"

"*I don't know.*"

Silenced, she glanced at his troubled face as they went on deeper into the park, crossing the empty Place du Carrousel, going toward the river —not stopping to look at the marvelous expanse of Paris spread out to their right: the lovely stretching gardens and splendid Champs Elysées, the looming, shadowed Louvre. It was as if they were walking across the moon.

As brightly as she could, Deirdre said, "I'll go to New York and bring Marcus back. I can work here."

"I can't. I can't even stay in France."

"Then we'll go someplace else."

He stopped and looked her full in the eyes. "Where? My friend, Gordon, went to Montreal, and he writes really upset letters."

She made a gesture of despair. "Evan, why are you being like this?"

"Do you know what you're talking about? You can't change your whole life."

Her chin thrust out, Deirdre summoned some of her old defiance. "You don't have the foggiest notion of what I can do."

He acknowledged this with a quick grin; then, serious again, he turned and started on toward the river. After a moment Deirdre followed after him.

Behind them a street-cleaning truck passed, slowly washing the Place du Carrousel, before going on to help prepare the rest of Paris for the coming day.

Catching up with Evan, Deirdre tried a different tack. Softly: "If you do wait a while, isn't there a chance that they'll see things differently?"

"An amnesty? For a deserter who went to Moscow? Don't hold your breath."

"Christ, you're so resigned! I can't stand it!"

He might not have heard her. "The war's almost history, Deirdre. People just want to bury the last ten years, like they never happened. And I don't blame them."

He reached out for her, to draw her close, but Deirdre moved away from him. For a moment he watched her, her slender neck above the black turtleneck, her hair blowing in the light dawn breeze. Finally: "How late do those planes take off?"

She answered neutrally. "I told you. I think they go all day."

As they crossed the river, going toward the Ile de la Cité, Deirdre pointed to the next bridge up. "See? Pont Neuf. It's the oldest bridge in Paris."

Blindly Evan looked in the direction that she pointed, and saw a bridge.

"There's St. Chapelle."

A slender Gothic church.

From the river a cold wind rose. The few other pedestrians—a young couple, a professorial-looking man—hunched their shoulders against the cold and stared at the odd Americans.

At the edge of the flower market, at Place Louis Lepine, Deirdre and Evan paused—completely oblivious to the display; the lines of dim greenhouses, the flowers that were being set out in the open spaces between. Now, in the early morning, there were only florists and a few thrifty housewives who had come out to buy.

"You understand what that life is like?" Evan earnestly asked. "You could wear out, or I could wear out. Or they could send in the Mounties."

She looked at him. "It's worth a try."

"I've seen perfectly nice people end up hating each other."

Deirdre nodded.

Needing room to breathe, Evan turned from her and went farther into the market. A handful of merchants were sweeping the sidewalk; others set out plants or gossiped over thermoses of coffee or flasks of red wine. Looking desperately about, Evan saw nothing at all.

Deirdre came up to him. "Look, I don't want to bug you."

He stopped walking.

She said, "I mean, you don't have to make up your mind right now." Then she closed her eyes for a moment against the madness of what she had just heard herself say.

Evan's voice was strangled. "Like when?"

Deirdre nodded hopelessly, and they moved on again, farther into the market. They walked between benches where flowers soon would be displayed and past huge displays that were already set out: weddings, funerals.

"You know," said Deirdre, "When I woke up this morning I had this dumb daydream. It's funny how we kid ourselves. I really had myself convinced that I could be a better person with you."

Evan winced but she went on.

"You know, Deirdre the virgin."

"Listen—uh—I think you better—just stay away from me for a minute."

"It's just a joke."

His voice was barely audible. "Not funny, McCluskey."

He plunged on ahead. Having left her behind, he slowed down to a walk. Unaware of anything around him, he went on along the sidewalk, until suddenly he did see something that made him stop and stare: a grim, dark, and imposing building. A squad of gendarmes and several police vans, visible through an archway to one side. The Prefecture of Police.

In front of the building a long line of people stretched halfway down the sidewalk. Foreigners: Algerians, American hippies, Scandinavians, Italian working men. All poor.

Evan moved slowly toward the prefecture, and, catching up with him, Deirdre followed. Together they watched that line of patient, shabby people.

At the head of the line a sign explained the mechanics involved in getting or renewing a work permit.

Evan turned to Deirdre, finally aware of her at his side. "Who are they?"

"I don't know."

"Lost your French?"

She didn't answer.

He went on. "They're some kind of aliens, aren't they? It's stamp-the-permit time."

She admitted, "Yes."

"I could smell it."

At that moment, from the courtyard of the prefecture the sound of police klaxons pierced the air, and the gendarmes moved back from the archway.

"You ever been in one of those lines?" Evan asked. "If you really want to feel like you're not an American." He reached for her hand. "Come on, let's try it for size."

With a shocked look at him Deirdre held her hands tightly together. "Evan—"

One of the gendarmes blew a whistle, terribly shrill in the yellow morning air, and a police van came barreling out of the archway. Deirdre stepped back for safety, and the van passed violently between them. Then another van tore out, between them, leaving distance and silence in its wake.

Across that distance they looked at each other.

26

BY MIDMORNING, the lobby of the Crillon was in business again: a flurry of arrivals and departures, rounds of impressive luggage. People standing around in expensive traveling clothes.

Picking her way through the people and their bags, a worried frown of concentration on her face, Barbara suddenly stopped. She looked and looked again and then cried out, "Deirdre!"

Deirdre was standing near the concierge's desk, waiting for something.

"Sweetie, where have you been?" asked Barbara. "The 'Marie-Claire' people want us to lunch, and I—"

But then she stopped cold—her mouth opened in surprise. She had not expected to see Evan again, and yet there he was standing at the desk, discussing something about his airline ticket with the concierge. He nodded his thanks to the concierge and moved away. Barbara raised a questioning eyebrow, but Deirdre only said "Hi."

Evan joined them and tossed a friendly "Hello there" to Barbara.

"Good morning." An even tone represented Barbara's attempt at cool.

To Deirdre, Evan said, "I can get a plane at eleven."

"I'll take it with you."

"You sure?"

"Yes."

Their hands met and for an instant clasped together.

Watching them, Barbara realized that something momentous—at least to them—was going on. She was also aware that for the moment they had forgotten she was there.

Evan remembered and turned to her uncertainly.

Barbara made it easier for him. Putting out her hand, she said, "Well, good-bye again. Have a good flight."

Evan thanked her. Then he moved in the direction of the elevators to allow Deirdre and Barbara a moment of privacy.

They looked at each other seriously; there was too much to say.

"I'll call you in New York," said Deirdre, and she reached out to touch Barbara's arm in a gesture of affection.

"Something tells me I should keep my mouth shut. Am I right?" Barbara's voice was full of concern.

Deirdre nodded gravely, and then she went over to join Evan, where he waited with her luggage and his knapsack. Barbara stayed at the concierge's desk, transacting business of her own: the lunch, an interview, her late afternoon flight, a cable to Charlie and the girls.

The first two seats of the 707 first-class cabin on the plane to New York were occupied by a heavily beribboned general and a colonel. The general read the financial page of the *Paris Tribune*; the colonel was reading *Playboy*.

"I was thinking of retiring next year." The general's accent was clearly that of someone from North Carolina. "Buy a little place near Southern Pines—that's the golfing part of my state. But the way the market's going, my pension isn't going to be worth a damn."

"Yes sir," said the colonel absently. He was from California and was somewhat tired of being addressed as a foreigner unfamiliar with the geography of the USA. Also, he had heard that remark or variants on it several dozen times. In fact, on occasion he had made it himself.

Farther back in the same cabin, Deirdre and Evan were in their seats—laps spread with magazines as yet unopened. So far they had alternated between snatches of intense conversation and periods of silence which in their hopelessness were fully as intense.

Deirdre asked, "How about your sisters? How do they feel?"

Surprisingly Evan grinned at that. "Well, that's sort of interesting. They cover a wide range. Margaret, she's the oldest, is most like my mom. She's puzzled and sort of hurt by the whole thing. And then there's Frances, the middle one—she's very much into some psychoanalytic thing, she gives me stuff about competing with dad. It's sort of hard to take."

Deirdre smiled. "Guess who's your least favorite sister." Then she asked, "How about the youngest?"

He frowned. "Ruth. She's just a kid. But she's really nice. You'd like her." He frowned again, experiencing a vague kind of inner pain. "She's really made me into some kind of hero," he said. "God, I can't seem to straighten her out. If I could see her, and we could talk—"

The magazines were replaced with trays of lunch: small filets and artichoke hearts, a French Beaujolais.

Evan asked, "You're not hungry?"

"Not very." She smiled over at him.

"Did you at least think you were in love with Ron?" he resumed.

"Maybe for an hour or so, every now and then. But then next hour I'd know I'd been kidding myself. I'm a pretty honest girl," she told him, somewhat wryly. At the same time she thought: I only *thought* I was in love with Derek, so I don't have to mention him now.

"I noticed," Evan said. "A very honest girl."

Green countryside appeared far below the plane. "Iceland? Newfoundland?" Deirdre asked.

"I'm not sure."

She picked at her food for a while, then asked, "Are there going to be a lot of creeps in gray suits waiting for you at the airport?"

"I doubt it. I'm not that important."

"Then what do you do?"

"I'm supposed to go to some office in the Federal Building." He hesitated. "I'll have a few hours. Can we go to your place?

"Marcus and my mother'll be there."

"I know. I'd like to meet them."

She waited for him to explain what he meant by that amazing statement, but Evan was peering beyond her, out of the window. "It must be Newfoundland. Means we're almost there," he told her.

27

AT A WINDOW OF an attractive townhouse in New York's East Seventies, a small boy and a middle-aged woman eagerly watched the street. A lumbering moving-van passed, momentarily obscuring their view. A taxi rushed past, nonstop. More cars. A taxi that stopped in front of their door.

A blonde girl got out. Deirdre. "Mommy!" Marcus raced for the front door.

Deirdre, and a strange young man. Puzzled, although not surprised—she had long ago got over being surprised by Deirdre—Mrs. McCluskey followed her grandson to the front door in time to see him rush out and into his mother's embrace. She went out after him and in her turn hurried over to kiss her daughter.

The young man was helping the cab driver with the luggage.

Deirdre said, "Wow, it's so great to be back— great to *see* you!" and she bent to hug Marcus again.

Then she turned to Evan, who had finished the bags and had been watching the excited homecoming. "And this is my friend, Evan Bonner. My mother and my son, Marcus."

Evan shook hands with them both; warmly with Mrs. McCluskey to whom he said, "I'm really glad to meet you"; gravely with Marcus. Then he followed Deirdre and her family into the house.

Almost immediately the room was strewn with presents, as Deirdre began to open boxes and bags. Sitting on the floor with Marcus she handed him the djellaba from Sidi-El-Boum, an ornate wooden cutlass, a leather pouch. There was a brilliant woolen stole for her mother and a large bottle of Joy from Paris.

Pleased, Mrs. McCluskey scolded her daughter. "You always buy so much—this house looks like Christmas morning."

Deirdre laughed at her. "You should see what Barbara is bringing back if you think I'm so bad."

She was a plain, kindly woman, Deirdre's mother. In her middle forties, she had done nothing to forestall the effects of time: no soothing creams or diets, no dyes or rinses in her graying hair. She wore what could only be called a housedress: a pink, rather shapeless wraparound. If she had missed having her husband around, she had never let it show, and the lines around her mouth bespoke control.

Evan got down on the floor with Deirdre and Marcus. Deirdre helped Marcus into the djellaba, and Evan adjusted the hood for him.

"You wear it like this," he told Marcus. "You can sneak up on people."

Teasingly he pulled the hood over Marcus's face, and Marcus laughed with delight.

Deirdre's apartment, which Evan barely had time to see, was both luxurious and beautiful. And comfortable: a huge soft sofa in gray suede lined one wall, and there were big chairs in patterned velvet, gray and rust and beige, and small chairs of brown leather and steel. At the end of the room long windows led into a small garden: a green oasis surrounded by skyscrapers.

The kitchen, where Mrs. McCluskey now went to make more coffee, was of dark wood and stainless steel and blue-and-white tiles from Portugal; the effect was warm and efficient. Deirdre joined her mother there; they moved easily around each other in the kitchen, getting together coffee and sandwiches. They both stopped from time to time to look through the open door at Evan and Marcus, who still played on the floor in the living room.

Mrs. McCluskey said quietly to her daughter. "Is he going to be here long?"

Deirdre bit her lip. "No, I don't think so."

"That's too bad."

Wise to her mother's ways, Deirdre asked, "Something on your mind?"

As her mother spoke out, some trace or shadow of Deirdre's face appeared on hers, some of Deirdre's defiance in her voice. "I like him," she said. "He's different from the men you know. More like the boys at home."

Deirdre looked at her mother, then with a rush of affection she suddenly hugged her.

Mrs. McCluskey was disconcerted. "Well he is—"

The sounds from the living room had stopped, and Deirdre and her mother watched Marcus, who was totally absorbed in examining the cutlass.

Evan was watching Marcus too, and Deirdre scanned his face: what future did he see for Marcus, or for himself? Impossible to read his expression, she decided.

Sensing too much attention being focused on him, Marcus became uncomfortable. Evan noticed and got down on his knees. He pretended to examine the cutlass and said: "Come on, I'll show you how to use that."

As Deirdre and her mother returned to their food preparations, Deirdre said, "Don't go to a lot of fuss. We sort of ate on the plane."

"There's ham and some turkey."

Deirdre shrugged happily. "Okay!" and she went back into the living room.

Evan, still down on his knees was dueling at Marcus with the cutlass.

"I got you!" Marcus cried out.

Evan grunted. "You sure did."

"I got you!" excitedly again.

But Evan had turned to Deirdre, who said, "My mother wants to feed you."

"Sure."

"Can we go to the park this afternoon?" Marcus

asked his mother, and turning to Evan, peremptorily he added, "You too."

Deirdre and Evan exchanged a look.

Evan said, "I'd like that."

Mrs. McCluskey bustled in, bearing a tray that was stacked with sandwiches, coffee, and cups. Refusing offers of help from both Evan and Deirdre, she put it on the coffee table, then distributed plates and sandwiches.

"This is the best ham I've had in—in years," Evan told her.

She acknowledged the compliment with a prim, pleased smile. "There's another kind of mustard, if you like."

"No, this is fine."

Marcus remained on the floor among his new treasures, still wearing the djellaba, picking up first the cutlass, then a miniature French car. Ignoring the boring adult conversation, he addressed Deirdre urgently: "Mommy, do you know what happened at school?"

"What, chief?"

"I built a train station, and Billy took the blocks. I kicked him."

Deirdre and Evan stifled an exchange of smiles, and she drew Marcus close to her. "That was pretty mean of Billy."

Evan watched Deirdre and her son, observing the similarity in their features, in their coloring. There had to be something of Ron in Marcus didn't there? Conscientiously looking for that something, Evan was struck with the inadmissible thought that Marcus very slightly resembled himself.

"Debby said it was the goodest station. He made it fall down. I hate Billy," Marcus announced.

"All right now, I think that's enough," Marcus's grandmother intervened.

"He took all my blocks."

Under cover of that exchange Deirdre leaned forward and spoke privately to Evan. "What time does that office close?"

"I don't know. Five o'clock, I suppose."

"I'm glad I kicked him," Marcus burst out.

28

DEIRDRE AND EVAN each held one of Marcus's hands as the three of them crossed Fifth Avenue and headed into Central Park. In his other hand Evan carried Marcus's ball; his knapsack was on his back.

Releasing their hands as they reached the park, Marcus ran ahead of them on a small path that took them deeper into the park. Then he took off from the path to climb a tiny hill.

Although Marcus was out of hearing, Deirdre spoke very quietly. "You know, Barbara's husband's a lawyer. Charlie. He has a lot of friends in Washington. In fact, I know some people too."

"I don't think it would help. The court-martials are pretty cut and dried."

She looked at him, wanting to ask, You're still going ahead with it?

Evan avoided the look; instead he watched Marcus, who at that moment ran down his hill and flung the ball at Evan. "Catch!"

Neatly Evan caught the ball, and threw it to Deirdre, who passed it on to Marcus. Marcus missed, and as he ran to retrieve the ball Evan and Deirdre exchanged a long, searching look.

She whispered, so that he could barely hear. "I shouldn't say this, but he looks the smallest bit like you."

"I noticed." He brought this out painfully.

"Let's play tag instead!" Marcus cried out.

"Okay, I'm it," and Deirdre tagged her son.

Marcus set out after Evan, who let him give a little chase by darting back and forth, shifting direction, just out of reach.

Finally, "Got you!" Marcus delightedly cried out.

Evan started after Deirdre, who ran away from him. But then, as he cornered her against a clump of trees, it was no longer a game. They both sobered and stared at each other apprehensively, both fearful of the impending, and possibly final, touch. *I just want you to touch me.*

To minimize the moment, Evan tapped her shoulder playfully. "You're it."

She, in her turn, attempted a smile.

"Come on, I want to go to the slides!"

They both turned to Marcus with a sort of relief. He took a hand from each, and they let themselves be led to his favorite slide.

The slide, which was very high, sat in a small play area near a cross street. The sounds of late-afternoon traffic intruded through the trees.

Marcus got up to the top of the slide, as Deirdre anxiously perched on a bench nearby.

Evan waited at the bottom of the slide. "Come on!"

But Marcus hesitated.

"Come on. I'll be right here."

Deirdre watched as Marcus came swishing down the slide, watched Evan smile at him.

Near the slide stood a large jungle gym, to which Marcus now ran triumphantly, and he started toward the top.

Deirdre got up and went over to stand beside Evan. "When I left he was still afraid to go all the way up."

He smiled down at her, but with pain visible in his eyes. "It's a pretty big one."

Marcus reached the top, beaming as he looked down at them. Deirdre and Evan raised their clasped hands over their heads in congratulation, and Deirdre called out, "Hey, you did it!"

As Marcus climbed down, which took a little time, on a single impulse Deirdre and Evan turned to each other. They both knew it was time: there was everything, and therefore nothing, to say.

Marcus ran up to Evan. "Will you push me on the swing?"

Evan hesitated.

"I'll push you," Deirdre said, and she took his hand and walked with him over to the swings.

Behind them Evan looked at his watch, to confirm what he already knew: almost five. He went over to get his knapsack, as Deirdre put Marcus in a swing and began to push him. Watching them, Evan picked up his knapsack.

After a moment he managed to force himself to approach them. Busy with the swing, Deirdre did not hear him come, and again he waited before he said, "Good-bye, Marcus."

Startled, almost incredulous, Deirdre turned to him. She stepped back from the swing and waited there.

As he began to slow down Marcus looked at Evan. He seemed not to know just what was going on, but he was not upset. "Good-bye," he said.

Evan came up to where Deirdre stood, and they stared at each other—once more, their faces, that had faintly the same shape, wore the same expression—haunted blue eyes staring into haunted blue.

Deirdre spoke first. "I'm not going to make any promises. In three weeks I may be in a mess again."

He didn't answer that.

She insisted. "I'm just not good at waiting for things."

"We'll see," he told her.

She faced him fully, said—suddenly, "I love you."

He reached for her, he held her very close, as she held him—for a long and intensely painful moment, until Evan broke free and started off, out of the playground.

Deirdre stood watching him go.

Marcus had drifted to a stop on the swing.

Deirdre went back to her son and began to push him again, as Evan reached the cross street and hailed a cab. Knapsack slung in first, he got in, not looking back to where Deirdre pushed Marcus slowly at first, and then higher and higher, against an April sky that began to hold the first shadows of an encroaching dusk.